AMUSINGS

Ian Jackson

Grosvenor House
Publishing Limited

Book cover illustration by K Taylor. (Design: plop!)

This book is published by
Grosvenor House Publishing Ltd
Link House
140 The Broadway, Tolworth, Surrey, KT6 7HT.
www.grosvenorhousepublishing.co.uk

A CIP record for this book
is available from the British Library

Paperback ISBN 978-1-80381-806-1
Hardback ISBN 978-1-80381-807-8
eBook ISBN 978-1-80381-808-5

To Mum and Dad

Thanks for everything

Contents

List of figures

Foreword

Professional writers spend much of their time trying to achieve greatness in their work, be it existential or commercial. Yet sometimes, the unfettered writing of someone from another field, unencumbered by ego and blind adherence to professional practice, strikes a visceral, emotional chord in the public arena. As a former writer in residence at a high security prison boasting a population of over a thousand clients housed at Her Majesty's Service, I occasionally came across naturally gifted writers who, at the swish of a pen, could evoke imaginarium and wit, more often than not, unbeknownst to the author. I would venture to say that Ian Jackson's writing appears to accomplish elements of this feat, with its prudent dissection of theme with a splash of hyperopic humour.

I first came across Ian over two decades ago when brought in as a writer on an infamous Japanese film project he was involved with. After two months of furious writing, I'd come up with a sixty-five-page treatment that quickly made its way to the top of the eponymous William Morris agency in the United States, whereupon I guess I had earned my right to dinner and a drink with Mr Jackson whose laid-back and carefree manner was a shot in the arm for a young writer and filmmaker struggling to make hay under a setting sun.

In 2016, Ian and his lovely wife, Barbara, left the UK for Australia after more than a quarter of a century under grey skies. A return trip curtailed by the Covid-19 pandemic was reinstated as soon as the barriers came down and I was extremely pleased to see that his energy and humour had not been washed away by the Sydney sun. Again, over dinner and wine, I reminded him of the time he allowed me to read one of his short stories which I'd suggested then be developed into a film. As we imbibed, the idea of publishing came to the fore. The rest is history, or should I say *his* stories?

So this writer is exceedingly glad that Ian acceded to the request of allowing publication of his writing and, moreover, I am also extremely pleased that his well-lived brand of social humour will be shared with so many more people.

Mark Norfolk

Preface

Amusing Musings. That sums up this book perfectly.

There is nothing heavy in these pages. There is no intention here to educate, lecture or convert. No philosophy. No theology. No politics. We all lead such a serious existence these days that I see it as my job to lighten things up a little.

So, the simple motivation behind my writing these stories is to make people smile. Over time, I've watched people read my stories and I see their faces light up when they hit a funny bit. That's extremely satisfying and addictive. Whenever someone smiles or laughs, I feel that the world is momentarily and marginally a better place.

I suspect that we are all a bit overwhelmed by the current goings-on, and irony can be a great shield. I hope that these stories capture my take on some of the major influences on our lives and on the consequential behaviour of our fellow human beings.

This book has only been made possible by the efforts of my good friend and editor, Mark Norfolk, who volunteered unexpectedly that he thought my stories were 'publishable'. I am very grateful for his efforts plus those of K Taylor, Petra Norfolk and Martin Kellard for their wonderful illustrations.

I have a dream that somewhere in the world in 3023, a person will come across *Amusings*, read it and laugh. I firmly believe that I will hear that laugh wherever I am.

Introduction

Hampstead Heath, London Borough of Camden, United Kingdom.

Deep within the heart of the borough, in the overpopulated city of London, the ancient heath teems with the shrieking activity of young rugby stars of the future, leaping and scrumming down. Amongst them, a child prodigy half-back possessive of extraordinary skills of speed and handling, well beyond the level of the adult international team.

A jobless man at the end of his wits is thrust into the limelight when he suddenly inherits a divine spiritual awakening that lifts his battered soul; and in a street nearby, an eager estate agent hatches a plot to re-invigorate the purposefully stagnant housing market, painfully unaware of a major, carbon-neutral, synthetic competitor on his doorstep.

And lurking in the shadows of the wooded lowlands, the Head Druid of a secret pagan organisation makes his most important announcement to his adoring disciples. It is an announcement of such great magnitude; it surely spells trouble for the future of humankind.

Yet, at the more salubrious village-end of the town, long-suffering wife Sarah finally makes a decision on a once-in-a-lifetime menu that will have serious consequences for her marriage.

Notwithstanding this domestic impasse, in the political sphere, an ambitious man hailing from a long-standing gentry family, waits patiently in line to meet the monarch on the greatest day of his and his family's life.

Meanwhile on the opposite side of the world, the Australian Senate convenes a secret emergency session to debate on a recent scientific discovery that will change the world and at the same time bring to ruin some of the globe's largest corporate companies.

From space, Hampstead Heath appears as peaceful as it was yesterday.

51.5608° N, 0.1629° W.

S

At long last, S has delivered the translation.

Since he retired to Krypton2, S prefers to be called Kal-El, his Krypton birth name, but, much to his chagrin, I call him, 'S'.

'Why do you persist in calling me *S*?' he complained.

'*S* for "Short",' I quip, but he doesn't get it.

You can see that he is not the sharpest tool in the box, but generally speaking, he's good company. He can be too earnest and self-righteous at times but he makes up for this with his entertaining tales from his time on Earth as a Superhero. He's also useful with obstinate screw tops, even though he's largely lost his superpowers nowadays.

Krypton2 is a satellite planet that avoided destruction when the original Krypton exploded. It became home to the survivors and, over the years, has grown into a thriving metropolis. S chose it as a retreat when things got unbearable for him on Earth.

Krypton2 is also where I've ended up but, until now, I had no idea where I came from. I knew that I was discovered as a baby in a crashed space capsule. The only clue to my origin was contained in a document found inside the capsule, written in an unknown script.

My adoptive parents tried for years to get this decoded and, in my adult years, I continued the quest with the same lack of success. So, you can imagine my surprise when recently, S asked rather sheepishly, if he could have a go. As a family friend, S has been a constant in my life and I felt I knew him well enough to think that such an intellectual pursuit would be beyond him. But as they say, nothing ventured, nothing gained. I remember hoping that he would not be embarrassed by his inevitable failure.

With low expectations, I had handed over the precious pages. Until that moment, no one had recognised the language, but S took one look and pronounced it to be 'English', with which he was obviously familiar. While I was simultaneously shocked and delighted, he took this calmly. Since then, he has been slowly translating the English into Krypton, impeded by both his poor Krypton and his dimness.

From his frustratingly intermittent updates, I now know that the document is, in fact, a letter from my father to me, written in sad anticipation of our permanent separation. It reveals that in events reminiscent of S's own experience, my father launched me into space to avoid some cataclysmic event. He had completed the letter only seconds before my departure.

When we last spoke, the precise circumstances which led to this decision were yet to be revealed and S had shared with me his understanding of the traumatic worldwide context of the time.

Ignoring the fact that, like me, he was abandoned by his parents, S had an idyllic childhood where, under the tutelage of his adoptive parents, he learnt to control his superpowers and use them for the fight against crime. Admirably, he adopted the credo: 'Truth, Justice and the American Way' which was to come back to haunt him.

As he told me this, it had seemed to me that this contest, the fight against crime, didn't require a lot of smarts on his part as his superpowers gave him an overwhelming advantage. Whatever the reason, S enjoyed decades of success and public adulation.

But there were greater forces at work that not even someone as powerful as S could resist.

Since his arrival, temperatures on Earth had been gradually increasing. Generations of ineffective politicians blocked attempts to address this climatic change with inevitable consequences. Low-lying island nations were inundated and their populations scattered, creating tension wherever they settled. Coastal towns and cities lost whole suburbs to the rising tides, putting intolerable demands on essential services. Food and water resources had come under increasing pressure and the rising temperatures ultimately resulted in worldwide famine and civil unrest. As governments struggled to control their people, the prospect of international nuclear war grew inexorably.

S says he watched in helpless horror as the world disintegrated around him. Presidents stole his mantra and twisted it. 'The American Way' became 'America First', and 'truth' and 'justice' became matters of loose interpretation. He couldn't tell the baddies from the goodies anymore.

The letter recorded my family's experiences through this tumultuous period. Somewhat perversely, they had prospered. My father had invested heavily in renewable energy and, in particular, battery technology, amassing a huge fortune. By the time I was born, my father was reported to be the wealthiest man in the world.

When delivered, this news had not sat comfortably with me. My father's gains had to be at someone's expense and it seemed unfair to have such wealth when the world was suffering. To be more precise, it seemed unfair to have great wealth *because* the world was suffering. S told me that even he was conscious that the gap between rich and poor was widening and there was a real danger of revolution unless the wealthy took steps to share their assets. They didn't.

The completed translation which S has just handed me explains my father's decision. S had been right. It was social unrest that forced my father's hand.

When the end came, it came swiftly, catching even my father by surprise. Governments foundered and anarchy reigned. Even with his money and influence, he could no longer guarantee the safety of his family, particularly as we were perceived to have benefitted from humanity's suffering.

They weren't ready when the vast mob broke through the perimeter defences of our family compound and they had only minutes to react. As a last resort, they had planned to escape by blasting themselves into space to find refuge on another planet. My family had been pioneers in private space travel and therefore 'had the technology'. But their preparations were incomplete when the rioters crashed through the front door, overrunning our security guards and only one small rocket was ready. I was a babe-in-arms and, in desperation, my parents decided to save me, sacrificing themselves.

The idea was that the capsule's ingenious support systems would keep me alive long enough to reach another planet. As I read this, it occurred to me that the odds of my landing safely somewhere inhabited, let alone inhabited by beings who were genetically identical to me, are inestimable. But there you have it. Comic book stuff. I couldn't help thinking that this must have been a low point in the history of responsible parenthood.

Eventually, I had arrived on Krypton2 where my life was very different from that of S's on Earth. Admittedly, we started out the same way with an intergalactic journey, followed by adoption by a loving, childless couple who bought us up as their own. While the Earth's alien environment bestowed superpowers upon S, Krypton had the opposite effect on me. The crushing gravity and thin, foreign atmosphere almost killed me when they took me out of the capsule and then proceeded to cripple me. Since then, I have spent my life on a sophisticated life-support system and there was absolutely no chance of me emulating his earthly Superhero antics.

But I had two things going for me. First, I inherited my father's intelligence and business acumen and second, all the locals were dumb as rocks (S was no exception).

It would seem that the original inhabitants of Krypton were an advanced civilisation or S wouldn't have had transport to

Earth, so I'm not sure how they came to regress. I'm assuming that, under pressure to escape the exploding planet, the intelligent ones made perfectly rational but incorrect choices and it was the idiots who survived.

Whatever the cause, there was no challenge to my rising to the top both academically and corporately, something which eluded my muscle-bound friend on Earth. What he did physically, I did mentally. Like S, I used my skills for the common good, perhaps unconsciously compensating for the sins of my father.

After I had read the story of my family and my narrow escape from certain death, there was one thing that still puzzled me.

I said to S, 'The chances of my surviving the journey were virtually zero, so what was my super-intelligent father thinking of? The only way I could have made it was if the craft was being guided in some way and this was impossible as my father didn't know of the existence of Krypton2, let alone its location.'

At that, S gave me a look that said 'and you think I'm the one that's stupid!' and pointed out the obvious. He had escorted me.

He patiently explained that my father had been a close friend for whom he had the greatest of respect. Far from being a greedy industrialist, my father was known for his philanthropy. S had gone to his aid on the evening of the uprising but it soon became apparent to both of them that the mob was irresistible. S could only subdue them by the use of extreme force and this was against his principles.

This crisis made S realise that his time on Earth was over. He was under pressure from all sides to join their cause but the situation was far too complex for him to make choices. Brute strength and nationalism were not the answer.

Standing with my father as he faced the dilemma of whether or not to blast me off the planet, S made the decision to return home. He offered to steer me safely to Krypton2 and thereafter to keep a protective eye on me as he anticipated the severe physical effect the Krypton environment would have on me.

He related how he had arranged for me to be adopted, had overseen my medical treatment and organised my education. Throughout my career, he had used his great influence to smooth my path. His natural humility prevented him from seeking my gratitude.

Such was my self-obsession, blinded by belief in my innate superiority, I had not noticed his guiding hand in my fortunes. It is true that I had faced adversity, but nothing could excuse this level of insensitivity.

His final act of loyalty was to wait until I had sufficiently matured before translating the letter. He wanted to be sure I could handle the truth and he wanted me to learn it in my father's words.

Stunned and embarrassed, I realised it was time to show Kal-El the respect he deserved.

UNNECESSARY ADVICE

86 The Mansions
Temple Fortune
London UK

Ms S Jacobson
Marie Curie Hospice
Lyndhurst Gardens
London UK

11 September 2023

Dear Sue,

Along with the rest of the family, I have been having difficulty coming to terms with your 'bombshell' news of last week, so I decided that the best thing I could do would be to try to make myself useful.

Casting around for ideas and given your new circumstances, I came to the conclusion that you might benefit from my vast knowledge of all things theosophical. You will have noticed that this is not something I've talked about a great deal in the past, but this is because I have always found it impossible to descend to the common level of debate.

Recent research puts Christianity as the outright favourite (at 2/1) for being the One True Religion, so that's a good starting point.

Having said that, I thought I'd do a review of the other religions to see if there was anything that might be appropriate in the current circumstances, some small gem that you could profitably adopt as an each way option.

I quickly discarded Rastafarianism on the grounds that it is patently ridiculous and you simply don't have the hair.

The other modern religions – Church of the Latter Day Saints and Scientology might have been refreshing but both required a lobotomy and I was looking for something less invasive for you in your condition.

So I have turned to Buddhism. The beauty of Buddhism is that it is philosophy rather than religion and elements of it can be incorporated into other religions without compromising their basic tenets.

Based on deep and detailed research over many minutes, I have come across the concept of निकास स्कोर, which is Nepalese for 'Exit Score'. Self-evidently, this is a way of rating each individual's method of leaving this 'mortal coil' and has applications in reincarnation, which I will explain.

There are two primary factors which determine the निकास स्कोर: timing (T1) and technique (T2). They both carry a maximum of 10 points.

With T1, an exit at 21 years of age or less scores zero and at 85 or more, 10. Based upon your expectations and your current age, your T1 will be around 6.

Being hung, drawn and quartered qualifies for a T2 of zero, while you would get a 10 for dying in your sleep in the arms of a Miss World or Mr Universe, depending upon your preferences and orientation. Your particular scenario which you've described as swift but uncomfortable deserves a 5.

So, on this assessment, you have an निकास स्कोर of 11.

So, what does this mean? Your निकास स्कोर helps determine the guise in which you will be reincarnated. An निकास स्कोर of 11 indicates that you will probably re-emerge as one of the higher primates, an orangutan most likely. If we could get you up to a 12, you would be upgraded to 'Melbourne Tram Conductor' which is much the same, except that you get to wear a uniform and be welcomed into cheaper restaurants. A 16 would earn you a role as a corporate CEO or Premier League football player.

If you are interested, there is a little-known option for increasing your निकास स्कोर. The Buddha left a secret code and anyone cracking it can have their score reviewed by properly certified individuals (like me). The code is 'NATWESTBSB12-10-18ACCN3786218 MARCUSEVANS'. Mysterious, eh?

I hope that this helps.

Love,

Marcus

PATIENCE

The CCTV watchers were disappointed when Albert stopped catching the train.

He had gradually drawn attention to himself by his punctuality and manner. Daily, he arrived at precisely 7.52am to catch the 7.58am and took up exactly the same position on Platform One.

Everything about him spoke of attention to detail and timeliness. His suits were pressed and his hair in immaculate condition with the length barely varying. His military bearing completed the picture of a deeply conservative man.

As is common with such personalities, Albert was intolerant of the failings of others. His patience was sorely tried by delay and imprecision. With increasing frequency, he would monitor the information displays to track the progress of the 7.58.

He would consult his watch regularly in an exaggerated manner, flinging his arm forwards to free his watch from his sleeve and snapping his arm back to bring the dial up to his nose.

Those watching from the signal control tower would greet each of these gestures with delight while keeping count.

The 7.58 would be sitting patient and unseen at a red light just outside of the station. When the count reached ten, they would change the signal to green, then the 7.58 would slide into view and Albert would board the carriage in a foul mood.

However, they had not seen Albert for several months now and had not been able to identify as reliable a victim to replace him.

Albert had taken early retirement.

As he explained to his wife, he just couldn't stand the commute.

She was as disappointed as the signalmen.

DRAMA ON HAMPSTEAD HEATH

I scuttle down Downshire Hill towards our rendezvous point on the Heath with my robe tucked under my arm. The urgent call had come earlier in the day and we rush from all over Hampstead to attend this meeting. We have no inkling of the purpose but the Imperial Grand Archdruid is not a man to be ignored. He has stronger powers than the rest of our Ruling Council put together and if displeased, has been known to use them without mercy.

This was not a usual meeting of the Heath and Hampstead Society and most of our members would be astounded if they knew about these proceedings. We, the inner circle, can trace our ancestry back to the Iceni and our families have lived continuously in Hampstead since those ancient times. We keep the old, secret traditions alive and our public face is the Heath and Hampstead Society through which we perform our good works.

It is late November in the early evening and darkness spreads across the Heath as I and my brothers make our way to the tumulus, known locally as Boadicea's Grave. We, of course, know the true origins of this mound which predate even our old queen.

By day, the Imperial Grand Archdruid is known as the President of the Society but tonight he reveals his true identity. He greets us at the mound and helps us negotiate the low fence. We don our ceremonial robes and take our appointed places amongst the trees and effectively disappear from view.

Our Master moves to the summit and the ancient trees tower around us like sentinels. We shiver with anticipation.

We know him to be a serious man and struggle to think what has caused him to summon us so abruptly. We are a secretive organisation and we do not like to draw attention to ourselves. There are severe risks associated with public meetings, even if they are held under the cover of darkness.

I know that some of our members are annoyed at the inconvenience but they dare not show it.

The darkness closes in around the circle like a thick cloud, separating us from the outside world. All external noise is muffled into silence. The temperature is dropping, the damp wind bites at our nostrils and we are grateful for our thick, grey, hooded cloaks.

He stands tall with his feet set defiantly apart as if braced for an attack. His hood is thrown back and his face shines in the light of the single guttering candle that he holds before him. His fashionable, proud locks wave menacingly in the wind as if a ghost were running her fingers through his hair. He holds his hands as if in prayer and his broad shoulders are hunched forward, framed by the swaying trees. We feel his strength radiating towards us in this ancient place.

His voice is pitched low so that we have to strain to hear him. The words echo around us and it is as if the trees themselves are speaking.

In language that is centuries old, he reminds us of our heritage and the oaths that bind us together, of our common beliefs and the deep secrets we share that can never be revealed to the outside world. He makes clear our obligations to Hampstead, Mankind and to the planet Earth itself. He lays before us the majestic accomplishments of our forebears, all to prepare us for the impending devastation. We can barely breathe as the sheer magnetism of his presence commands our total attention.

The pitch of his voice rises and falls and finally, barely audibly, he mutters the words that strike fear in our hearts and blasts our minds.

'I think I'm going bald.'

WAITING
ROOM
The Times

THE FAITHLESS HEALER

PLEASE RETURN WHEN READ

I've had so many people ask me why Ernie and I are running this business that I've decided to document the whole saga and leave copies for you, the customers, to read at your leisure.

Please return this when you've finished with it so others may have the pleasure.

It all started soon after Julie left me and Blackie, our cat. Blackie is actually white, his naming being an example of my (self-defined) ironic sense of humour which Julie said was one of the reasons she was departing. But she said the main reason was that the two of us, Blackie and I, spent more time out of the apartment than in it and, if she was going to be lonely, she 'may as well go and do it properly on her own'. I concede there's some logic to this.

I'm not sure where Blackie was going at night, but I was working long hours at the bank and the Holly Bush pub around the corner was an irresistible refuge which waylaid me on the way home. Not very considerate of me I have to admit.

To make matters worse, I was made redundant shortly afterwards and my future was looking particularly bleak.

I've always felt that the consequent trauma triggered the change in me, even though multiple government psychiatrists subsequently diagnosed to the contrary.

And what was that change?

I could heal. Simply by being within a few feet, I could cure people's illnesses. This is absolutely true as verified by subsequent government trials. At the time, I thought I was going mad.

Some would call it 'faith healing' but there was no 'faith' involved in my case. No religion, no guardian angels, no auras, no trances. I was the original 'faithless healer'.

The first inkling I had involved Blackie.

It was a Friday night, and I was vaguely watching TV when Blackie bolted through the cat door, trailing blood and wailing in pain. He'd obviously been fighting the ginger tom from next door and lost again. I rated Blackie the second-best fighter in Hampstead on the basis that he'd had around fifty fights and came second every time.

I scooped him into my arms and held him tightly in an attempt to calm him down. I could feel him quivering in fear and then he suddenly relaxed. I thought he'd died on me but no, he began to purr.

I was then able to put him back down on the floor so that I could examine the damage. Fearing the worst, I gently felt down his right side. Absolutely nothing. No wounds. No bleeding. I checked his left side. Again nothing.

Blackie started to take an interest, but he could find no cause for concern either. He looked at me with a bemused expression and headed for the kitchen and his dinner.

Somewhat confused, I went to bed early as I had arranged to meet my fellow allotment gardener, John, down the road at Branch Hill allotments the next morning.

I was tilling away when John appeared and crossed his plot next door to greet me. To my surprise, he performed that age-old slapstick trick of standing on an upturned rake head and smashing himself in the face with the handle. I'd never seen this done in real life before and found it genuinely very funny. Suppressing my laughter, I ran to his aid, lifting him up from his knees and holding his face in my hands to examine the damage. Blood was pouring from his nose, which had taken on a most peculiar shape. Imagine a lump of dough which had been hit by a rolling pin. As I watched, the blood stopped, and his nose carefully rearranged itself into its normal configuration. Imagine a lump of dough which hasn't been hit by a rolling pin. John saw none of this because he had his eyes tightly shut.

That decided it. I had to seek advice on what to do from our resident Hampstead guru, my dear friend, Ernest, the oracle of Hampstead. Ernest has had every job imaginable (butcher, miner, university lecturer, swan-upper) which he feels gives him his right to take up residence in the Holly Bush and dispense wisdom in exchange for the occasional pint. Every eccentric has his unique insignia and Ernie's is a Coat of Many Stains from which he will not be parted. He thinks it gives him an air of stately authority; others would think it an affectation.

He's at the Holly every Saturday from around 5pm so, later on that day, I set myself up at the bar and waited for his arrival. After I'd briefed him on these magical events, he was impressed but sceptical and needed more evidence. Conveniently, he had a small scratch on his left hand as a result of an altercation with a squirrel which was trying to retrieve a nut he'd stolen. (Don't ask.) Thus, I was able to give him a live demonstration. The scratch disappeared. That convinced us both that I wasn't hallucinating.

Together, we hatched a plan. Step 1 was me buying us another pint. (I've often puzzled over how all of our plans since time immemorial have involved my buying a round as Step 1, but never mind.) Step 2 was to ambush our dear friend and local doctor, Ben, who always dropped into the pub for a 'reorientation' pint on his way home from surgery.

As expected of a medico, Ben required more convincing than Ernie. On questioning, by way of a demo subject, the only thing he had to offer was a mildly embarrassing medical condition of a personal nature which was resisting his treatment. I was able to weave my spell and 'lo and behold it was fixed, without the laying on of hands, I'm relieved to say.

Returning from the Gents, we agreed on a new plan. To save time, we adopted the usual Step 1. Step 2 was that I would turn up in his waiting room on Monday morning and hover about. The idea being to assess what sort of conditions I could cure. This was not very scientific, but it was a start. (Ernie and I had a secret plan with a different Step 2 (but the same Step 1) which we did not share with Ben.)

Monday morning found me lurking behind a copy of *The Times* while surreptitiously observing the patients as they sat and then filed into his office. After a couple of hours, Ben came out to report his findings.

Every patient who was presenting for the first time would explain their symptoms to him but when he tested for those symptoms, they didn't exist. They had already been cured.

For patients who were already under treatment, the story was similar. Whatever their stage of recovery when they arrived that morning, they were fully healed by the time they reached Ben.

This was true for a whole variety of common complaints: infections, broken bones, wounds, heart failure. He couldn't test immediately for more complicated problems such as cancer, but this data satisfied Ernie's and my needs for our secret plan.

Ben banished me from his surgery on the grounds that he would have no patients if I stuck around for too long.

Back in the Holly that evening, Ernie and I decided on our business strategy. We would open a Harley Street clinic; the beauty of a Harley Street address being that folk assume that you are highly qualified while all it indicates is that you can afford the rent and probably overcharge.

We would only treat simple ailments as proven by Ben to avoid attracting too much attention and causing controversy: I've never seen anyone prosecuted for faith healing and I think it's because they are very careful about their claims. In particular, we were definite that we would not restore missing limbs, this being the ultimate test of the faith healer (or faithless healer in my case). Not that I knew whether I could or not and I wasn't aiming to find out.

Ernie had reluctantly agreed to shed his Coat of Many Stains, don a white coat and act as practice manager. His job was to screen clients to make sure their problem wasn't too complicated so as to maintain our low profile. If I'd known what was going to eventuate, I would have confiscated his hip flask.

All went well until the 'Martin Short' incident which everyone has heard about. It was all over the national press for weeks. Martin is famous. He is the greatest snooker player of all time. He has won multiple world championships and his engaging personality has made him a national treasure. The whole country mourned with him when he lost his right hand in an unfortunate accident. He was playing a match on a coin-operated billiard table when it swallowed one of his pound coins without dropping the balls. In attempting to fish it out, he cut his hand, developed gangrene and his hand was amputated, earning him the sobriquet 'One Pound Short'.

Martin was cunning: too cunning for Ernie. He knew of our policy not to restore limbs, so booked under an assumed name and wore a very convincing prosthetic which got him safely past Ernie who was halfway through his flask. As he walked into my consulting room, he deftly removed the prosthetic and offered me his stump for a handshake. I didn't notice because I did as my father instructed me and was looking him straight in the eye when my hand felt the stump. Before our eyes, his hand regrew from chubby baby size to full grown within a couple of minutes. I had just passed the faith healer test albeit inadvertently.

Things stayed quiet for a time but then Martin resumed his snooker career and regained the world championship in quick order. In his victory interview on the BBC, he acknowledged my role in his recovery, ignoring our confidentiality agreement. The game was up.

The day after the interview, the queue outside our clinic stretched down Harley Street all the way to the Euston Road and beyond. The extremely religious were hailing me either as the new Messiah or the Devil Incarnate. It wasn't long before the first fight broke out between differing theologists and by mid-afternoon rent-a-mob turned up and full-scale rioting took off with windows smashed and cars burned.

For our safety, Ernie and I were evacuated by police helicopter from the roof above the clinic.

By this time, the Emergency Cabinet, COBRA, had been convened and the prime minister was directly in control of operations. It was decided to take us to a safe house on the outskirts of London until things settled down.

The helicopter plopped down in the grounds of an impressive manor house surrounded by high security fences and patrolled by armed guards who were up to their armpits in Dobermans. We began to feel safe. Ernie stayed close to me in case he needed quick repairs.

The PM herself arrived to assess the situation and agree a plan of action. Ernie was most put out when he learnt that Step 1 wasn't the usual. He was regarded as a security risk especially when drunk so was given the choice of going home and remaining sober or staying with me and having free access to the bar. He chose the latter which provided me with convivial company for the duration.

Specialists were flown in to test me and my powers in a much more scientific manner than we had done with Ben. They could not identify the source of my powers and would not accept my argument that it was Julie's fault. In terms of scope, they could find no limit to my powers. The trials went very slowly because we kept being distracted by my having to treat the researchers' close friends and relatives. I suspected a conflict of interest but was told this was normal.

There was a proposal that they should test me to see if I could raise the dead as some bright spark thought it would be a good thing if we had Churchill back. Thankfully, the Health Research Authority which is responsible for ensuring ethical research put a quick end to that. If we'd gone down that path, Churchill may have been the least of our worries.

Ernie and I did our own research on the side with a lab rat, and it worked. We kept him as a pet and called him Lazarus. He's still alive today which is a bit worrying. It might be permanent. We're keeping an eye on Lazarus. He might be valuable.

The authorities were at a loss as to what to do with me and, to a far lesser extent, Ernie. The only problem with Ernie was that the bar bill was a lot higher than they'd budgeted.

It was suggested that I be co-opted to the National Health Service to treat the public, but as I had to be in close proximity I had a limited capacity to, say, a few hundred a day if they moved quickly and there was a lot of debate over how priorities would be decided. Who would be first? The richest, the sickest, the most valuable to humankind, the British, lottery winners, the test-cricket captain, the most charitable, the most intelligent? World wars have been fought over less.

And security would be a big problem. If the religious mob got hold of me, I'd either be crucified or sanctified.

The PM solved the problem by appointing herself as the setter of priorities. There's nothing so efficient as a strong leader motivated by self-interest.

Initially, she went for the low-hanging fruit, meaning regular visits to Buckingham Palace, Westminster, the White House and the houses of the Great and the Good; anywhere where the PM could score brownie points to strengthen her tenuous hold on office. They blindfolded me for these sessions, so I never knew the identity of the patient or their ailments. I decided it was best that I didn't know. If I did know, by now there'd be a target on my back.

Soon enough, the PM worked out that there was negotiating power to be gained by bringing me to the table in delicate political situations where one of the parties was seriously or preferably terminally ill, sometimes by arrangement. She became adept at discreetly trading my healing services for concessions in some very high stakes plays.

Whilst the Official Secrets Act prevents me from revealing too many details of my contribution, I will point out that, while I was detained in the safe house, the Colombian drugs trade was terminated, the Middle East crisis was resolved, and, perhaps most importantly, England won the soccer world cup for the first time since 1966. The PM also won the lottery but that's not public knowledge.

This was our life for about a year. Me going off on 'projects' with the PM, the researchers prodding, poking and sampling and Ernie sitting at the bar in his Coat of Many Stains.

Then the unthinkable happened and it couldn't have happened at a worse time.

The PM and I were in Saudi Arabia in negotiations with a very senior and terminally ill Prince.

The PM had reached agreement on a package of reforms to transform women's rights in the Kingdom in return for his being cured.

My moment of glory came and I stepped forward to perform the miracle... and nothing happened.

I had lost my powers just as quickly and easily as I had acquired them.

This cost the UK a lucrative arms deal and several billion in other trade, not to mention the mass disappointment of the world's female population. The PM's credibility was shattered and she lost the next election. She stopped sending me Christmas cards.

Ernie and I became irrelevant and retreated to Hampstead and our old lives, forgotten by all. Well, not quite our old lives as I didn't have a job and the Harley Street profit had been spent on compensation for the damage caused by the riots. Things were getting desperate again.

We spent many hours in the Holly Bush trying to find a way out of our dilemma but couldn't seem to get past Step 1. Mind you Step 1 had its compensations. Then one night when Ernie was very low and slumped on his bar stool in his Coat of Many Stains, I was moved to put an arm around him in a genuinely compassionate gesture and an amazing thing happened. The stains on his coat miraculously faded away and his coat was restored to its original glory.

'My God,' said Ernie, 'you can dry clean!'

So that's how Ernie and I became the proud owners of the curiously named 'Faithless Dry Cleaning'.

And to top it all off, Julie came home. Said she missed my 'sense of humour' and Blackie of course. Ha!

DAY DREAMING

Today was a bad day.

School was great until Miss Granger's lesson when she caught me daydreaming and told me off in front of the class.

'If you hadn't done so well in the exams, young Charlie, I'd give you a detention.'

It got worse when I was jumped by Geoff and his gang. They called me all sorts of names: 'dreamer', 'nerd', 'teacher's pet' and others I didn't understand. I wish I had some friends or even my own gang to help me fight back.

I raced away with hot tears running down my cheeks.

'Slow down!' Rupert said. But I didn't.

Flying around the corner into the High Street, I smashed into a crowd.

'What's happening?' I asked a man, tugging on his sleeve. He looked a bit scared.

'Young woman's been mugged,' he answered and pointed at a kid escaping on a scooter with a handbag.

My head still hurt from the beating and as I stood wondering what to do, Rupert said, 'Quick, use your mobile!'

The phone had come from Dad with strict instructions that it only be used in emergencies. 'I don't want you running up huge bills talking to your friends, Son,' he'd said, looking at me hard. *As if.* But I said nothing.

Nevertheless, I couldn't make the call to the police. I had lots of excuses: 'They'll never take any notice of a seven-year-old kid', 'I don't know what he looks like "cos of his helmet"', 'I can't read the number plate'. . . I felt totally useless as always and started to cry.

'No, no, Charlie, I meant use the special function!' shouted Rupert when he saw me blubbing.

The special function!

In the excitement, I'd forgotten that I'd secretly modified the phone for my own protection. I slid open the battery compartment and found the red button hidden inside.

Taking careful aim at the scooter, I fired. A brilliant blue ray flashed up the High Street blowing the rear tyre and throwing the rider into the street where some men grabbed him.

My heart swelled with pride as the crowd clapped loudly and I just knew that I would be a hero at school tomorrow.

But then Rupert spoiled things.

'In your dreams, Charlie! You made up that last bit.'

'Sorry, Rupert.'

'And while we are on the subject of dreaming, you realise that I'm not real, don't you, Charlie, like your parents have been telling you?'

'I-I guess so. . .'

'And you'll soon grow out of me, won't you?'

'Yes, but not yet! Please Rupert, not just yet–'

But he went. Just like that.

Tomorrow, I'll have to go to school alone.

I think it'll be another bad day.

A DISCREET CONVERSATION AT WHITES

The Attorney General arrived late for our dinner engagement.

I had expected this as he had been busy obtaining a last-minute injunction banning the BBC from broadcasting a story about the 'cash-for-honours' inquiry, a controversy that threatens to bring down the Labour government.

He was intrigued to know why I, a grandee of the Conservative Party, wished to dine with him but I kept him guessing until coffee. Unbeknownst to him, we share a problem over this 'cash-for-honours' nonsense, a practice that has been common for hundreds of years with few ill-effects in my opinion.

A little bird has been whispering in the ear of the constabulary, informing them about irregularities with recent appointments to the peerage, causing consternation in Downing Street. The identity of this dangerous bird is known to us because we have been watching him closely for a very long time.

Normally, we would take great delight in the discomfort of Messrs Blair and Company. The demise of their government is a crisis for them, an opportunity for us.

But this time unfortunately, we are playing for much higher stakes. Our little bird has even more damaging information dating back sixty years, that, if divulged, could bring down the monarchy – an absolute catastrophe!

Of course, I couldn't be entirely frank with him as he is from common stock – Quarry Bank School, I ask you! This meant being a touch disingenuous but us lot are experts in this field and it's become second nature.

I had deliberately chosen to meet him at my Club for reasons of confidentiality and home advantage. Where better to hide than in the open and among alert friends?

We enjoyed a fine meal, some excellent wine and polite conversation then retired to the library. This splendid room has played host to many a quiet, powerful conversation that has altered the destiny of men and countries alike and tonight it would fill this role again. The looming, polished bookshelves guarded us and our privacy as effectively as the Household Cavalry. I feel at home here just as my forefathers did before me and now it was important for me to appear relaxed. Conversely, I hoped it would put a man of his background at a disadvantage.

He had been suppressing his curiosity but when I revealed that I had useful information about his 'bird', his surprise and interest were palpable. Quickly, I imparted the facts that would permanently destroy the credibility of the informant and put the current matter to rest. It was a puzzled but grateful Attorney General who departed at speed.

This has been a damned inconvenience and if that interfering bird fails to get the message this time, we will take direct action as we did with Lord Lucan.

A drastic measure no doubt but God forbid that it ever gets out that Prince Philip paid Churchill to arrange his marriage! That would truly be the end of us.

HAM AND EGGS

On Friday, it was all over when her husband requested the same lunch he has had for ten years. It was the last straw.

Sarah was bored to death with her marriage and it was driving her to distraction. For years now, she had thought of doing this. Now it was time to act.

She sat on the bed reading *How to Plan a Divorce*, lent to her by her concerned friend, Prudence. Many-times-married Pru was an expert and never short of advice. It was Pru who had made Sarah realise how unhappy she was. Without Pru's encouragement, she would have been unable to confront Mark when he came home for lunch.

Her dress was the colour of wet slates, matching her mood. Her racing pulse betrayed her fear.

Bravery, she knew, was often underrated. She recalled a particular phrase her mother had once said 'Nothing ventured, nothing gained' and took heart.

Beyond the garden wall, there was a school. It was early afternoon and she could hear the children playing during their lunch break. This was a poignant reminder of the disappointment at being childless. Perhaps this was the root cause of her unhappiness.

She heard him open and close the garden gate and walked hesitantly into the entrance hall, catching her forlorn reflection in the mirror. The mirror was set in a gold frame, and she remembered the day he had bought it for her, saying, 'You're so beautiful, Darling. I want to preserve your reflection forever.'

She'd been deeply touched.

An unsuspecting Mark greeted her with a kiss when she opened the door and surprisingly presented her with a gift – a very small, very cute cocker spaniel puppy. Her heart and her resolve melted in an instant.

'I thought you might welcome some company,' he said.

They had ham and eggs for lunch again.

As Sarah played contentedly with Venus, she thought that she would make Mark ham and eggs for the rest of his life with pleasure.

When an efficient Prudence checked in later, she found Sarah in a combative mood.

Before Pru could open her mouth to express her disappointment and dismay, Sarah said, 'If you say even one word. . . '

She threw the divorce guide out of the window, just missing Pru's head as she ducked.

U.S.
Airspace
BORDER FORCE
USA

NOTES FOR THE AUSTRALIAN SENATE INQUIRY INTO THE GRAVITY PROJECT

Thank you for your unexpected invitation to give evidence before this Senate Inquiry into the finances of the Gravity project. Of course, I would have appreciated more notice, but so be it. I'm glad to have a chance to explain what has happened.

I initiated Gravity before I became the Minister for Energy and Climate Change. It was whilst I was still the Chief Scientist, a role to which I had been appointed a year earlier by the Prime Minister.

Although prestigious, the position of Chief Scientist has limited powers as I had found to my frustration. In particular, I led an inquiry into climate change policy and made recommendations, supported by all stakeholders, only to see my report rejected by the government due to pressure from a far-right minority. On reflection, this episode had put me in a vulnerable frame of mind when Frank Gilmore got in contact. I suspect that, ordinarily, I would have ignored him as we get a constant stream of crackpots knocking at the door. This started the chain of events which has led to my appearing before you today.

I don't know what subterfuge Frank used to get around my formidable secretary but, once he had me on the phone, he wasted no time telling me that he had made a scientific discovery which would dramatically cut carbon emissions and was of such importance that it would change the course of human history. I realised that this was probably nonsense but my morale was low, as I have explained, so I arranged to meet him the following week. He stipulated one condition, to which I agreed, namely that there would be no photographic record made. The significance of this only became apparent much later.

Frank appeared to be quite unremarkable. I'd had my staff do a little research and they reported him to be of middle age, middle income, middling height and weight. He'd had a quiet career in the Queensland Public Service, had no known interests and few friends. And he certainly had no scientific training which cast doubt in my mind over the existence of his 'world-changing' invention. He was reported to be a gentle, introverted character so his reaching out to me was unusual behaviour.

However, there turns out to be something quite different about Frank when you meet him in person. It is his eyes and it's hard to explain. When Frank engages you in eye contact, he controls your attention; you have the feeling of being nailed to the spot. It is a truly weird sensation and as will become clear, it is relevant to your deliberations.

At our first meeting, Frank made himself comfortable in a chair opposite me at my desk, after having checked that there were no cameras in operation. Frank then explained why he had insisted on this proviso. If knowledge of his discovery leaked, he felt his life would be ruined. He was a quiet man, leading a quiet life and he wanted it to remain so. He was happy to do his bit for the country and humanity, but not at the expense of his privacy. At the time, I didn't consider this to be odd.

In the intervening days, my enthusiasm had waned significantly and I was keen to get this over and done with as quickly and politely as possible so I cut straight to the chase and asked him to tell me about his discovery.

He said he'd do better than tell me, he'd show me.

To my great astonishment, he then levitated out of his chair and flew around the room before settling down again with a smile of self-satisfaction.

He explained that he had only recently become aware of this ability and had no idea how he accomplished it, so he wasn't sure if he could teach the trick to others. If this problem could be overcome, it didn't take the genius of a Chief Scientist to see the implications. My mind swirled with the possibilities.

Depending on how fast and how far people could fly, their reliance on local transport would be eliminated or seriously curtailed, resulting in a huge drop in carbon emissions as Frank had foretold. It seemed to me that the clean energy future we all hoped for had just got a lot closer.

But it also occurred to me that this prospect did not come without challenges. The transition would have to be managed with great care as the personal transport industry in all of its forms would become obsolete or, at least, severely scaled down with potentially devastating economic consequences.

And what of national security and law and order? Borders would become meaningless as people moved in large numbers between countries at will. Building walls would be pointless. This could lead to anarchy as governments lost control of their populations.

While I was still digesting the import of his remarkable demonstration, Frank made it known that he was looking for adequate payment for his cooperation and by 'adequate' Frank meant 'substantial'. He knew he was in a strong negotiating position as the value of his knowledge was inestimable, both in financial and power terms. Economies could be ruined, fortunes made and wars fought as a result of this. This was a fantastic opportunity for Australia to take a leadership position in the world.

With Frank still present, I called the Prime Minister on a secure line. He quickly understood the magnitude of the situation and the strategic value of Frank's knowledge but also of the personal danger Frank was in if knowledge of this leaked, unconsciously reinforcing Frank's own concerns. As you know, the PM is nothing if not decisive and, within an hour, Frank was accommodated in a nearby 'safe house' under the protection of the Secret Service. He was also considerably richer with a contract for cooperation of eye-watering proportions; the details of which I'm sure form part of your inquiry. We code-named the project, Gravity, and it was assigned the highest level of security.

We assembled a team of experts from the fields of science and medicine and Frank was subjected to every conceivable test to establish how he was able to fly. A hangar at Fairbairn Royal Australian Air Force Base was commandeered for Frank to demonstrate his flying technique in privacy. Apart from the unnerving penetration of his gaze which everyone noted, these experts could find nothing unusual about Frank which would explain his aerodynamics. While Frank was sympathetic to their plight, he seemed content enough to cooperate, as his bank balance ballooned.

After several months, the team came to me to confess that they were making little headway. They complained that being unable to film was severely restricting the analysis of their research. Given the amount of money that Frank was being paid, I decided that a little flexibility was justified. I gave permission for the next flight session to be covertly filmed on the condition that the file was to be delivered to me without being viewed. I would make the decision as to its relevance to their work.

They rigged a remote-controlled camera high up in the rafters of the hangar, filmed Frank in flight, retrieved the camera and delivered it to me, contents unwatched, as agreed. I had back-to-back meetings dealing with the aftermath of the rejection of my climate change report so it was a few days before I had a chance to watch the film. I was in a depressed state when I did so but, even so, what I saw blew me away.

Frank couldn't fly.

That's right. Frank couldn't fly.

The film showed the team looking up into thin air, tracking an invisible object while Frank relaxed in an armchair, looking on. I was astounded for a second time. No wonder he had insisted on no filming.

So Frank Gilmore was a master of delusion and an imposter, seemingly employing some form of mass hypnosis. This was potentially very embarrassing so I decided to keep it to myself while I decided what to do. I advised the team that there was nothing of interest on the camera and told them to carry on as best they could. They were not pleased but that didn't concern me. My hopes for a quick solution to global warming had been dashed.

The next day, I summoned Frank to my office and confronted him with the evidence, at all times avoiding eye contact. I educated him on the severe penalties associated with defrauding the government. He had no choice but to confess and he sat, contritely, waiting to learn his fate. He probably had the power to take control of me and the situation but he was too timid.

In short, we cut a deal.

Overnight, I had come up with a plan to use Frank's unexpected talents to deliver sensible climate change policy. We would close down the Gravity project on the basis that the skill was not transferable. I got a fair amount of flak for this but the experts backed me up and eventually everyone moved on.

Frank agreed to help me with a new project, getting me elected to the Senate. As you will be aware, Frank had made many millions in the short time Gravity had been active and didn't need to return to his job. He became my policy adviser, attending all meetings and rallies with me and using his powers of delusion and influence to convince all and sundry of my fitness for office.

It was a year to the next election and, by the time it came around, I had secured the number one position on the Senate ticket in Queensland for the Prime Minister's party and was duly elected. With Frank beside me, I have had no difficulty engineering my desired Cabinet appointment as Minister for Energy and Climate Change and then in getting my climate change policy implemented. This has broken the deadlock which was damaging the environment, not to mention Australia's international reputation. As a team, Frank and I have had a global impact for the betterment of the planet. For me, the end justifies the means. I'm happy, Frank's happy and the Earth's happy.

It is just a shame that the Auditor General decided to investigate the expenses of Gravity without my knowledge, leading to this Senate Inquiry.

As I said at the outset, I'm glad to have had the opportunity to get this off my chest and now let me introduce Frank who would like to say a few words. I'm sure he can clear things up for you.

THE REHEARSAL

'Jane, please come over here and help me repack this. We have another rehearsal this afternoon,' requested a windswept Elizabeth.

The others in the bridal party followed her firm lead in a slightly bemused manner. They worked earnestly in pairs with the experienced guiding the novices.

'I can't go through with this. I've had enough,' bewailed Jane.

Jane slumped down on the nearest pile of equipment, a picture of dejection.

Elizabeth settled down beside her in what she hoped was a comforting gesture and resisted the temptation of putting her arm around her in case it was misinterpreted.

'Oh, come on. I can understand that this is a real challenge for you but you're just being a spoilsport.'

'"Spoilsport", you're calling me a "spoilsport". That's very unfair. The only sport I should have spoiled was her father's when he insisted on trying for a boy for the fifth time. I blame him for all of this.'

'But Jane, you have to remember that this is your family's fifth wedding and Ruth has set her heart on doing something different.'

'I wouldn't call this *different*. I'd call it *suicidal*.'

'What's wrong with a quiet wedding in Kew Gardens like Susan's? Or the lovely gentle affair we had in Hampstead for Louise? When I drew the line at five children and Robert realised that he would never have a son, he tried to turn Ruth into one. The consequences are obvious. No offence meant.'

'None taken, but now it's you who is being unfair. Ruth has turned out to be a fine person and certainly one of the best recruits we have ever had. Whatever upbringing her father gave her, it has paid handsome dividends.'

'Well, you would say that, Elizabeth, wouldn't you? To be frank, Ruth has always been a huge disappointment to me.

My other daughters were real girls. Ruth was different. She wasn't interested in dolls or dresses and other feminine things. No, Ruth was the be-jeaned climber of trees and player of football. I just don't understand her. I couldn't believe it when she joined the army.'

'That is as it may be, Jane, but we have to get on with our preparations.'

'I told you. I'm not going to do it. I look absolutely ridiculous in this outfit. Small rotund mothers-of-the-bride should be allowed to wear a nice floral dress with a pert hat and sit demurely in the front pew, doing nothing more adventurous than kneeling in prayer. Why is she doing this to me?'

Jane was still puzzling over this the next day as she hurtled towards earth at terminal velocity, a reluctant participant in the world's first freefall, gay wedding ceremony.

'Well, Jane, all the training paid off in the end. You did very well.' Elizabeth congratulated her on landing.

'Are you saying that to me in your role as parachute instructor or "groom"?' came the acid response.

Jane tottered off in the direction of the reception in the Parachute Regiment Officers' mess, looking every inch the martyr.

WORLDS APART

Monday 9th October 2023 Earth Time

This will be my penultimate journal entry as we are expecting instructions to return home any time now. It takes several years for an exchange of messages with our base station on the other side of the galaxy, so patience is called for.

Our mission here was to assess the short- and long-term threat that Earth presents to our civilisation.

Simply put, our conclusion is that there is no foreseeable threat due to the character flaws of the dominant species. We advised our superiors of this in our last report, together with some tentative recommendations on actions we might take before we leave. As I said, we are awaiting a response.

Of all the planet's lifeforms bar one, humankind, show themselves to be primitive, lacking in self-awareness and with minimal communications capability. They have either been enslaved by other humans or merely exist at their pleasure.

On an individual basis or in small groups, humans appear to be generally courteous, law-abiding and considerate and bump along together quite happily.

However, when organised into large groups, they take on a different character, becoming paranoid and aggressive. Herein lies their weakness which eliminates them as a threat.

As a race (and oddly they don't see themselves as one race), they face multiple existential challenges, but they are unable to put together any coherent responses, placing their medium-term future in extreme jeopardy.

The 'race' issue is very interesting. We see it as Nature's design fault. Unlike us, they have the serious disadvantage of being monochrome with only a small number of variants at that, namely black, brown, yellow and white. This makes it all too easy at a group level to ascribe negative traits, motives and deficiencies to those of a different colour, learning to hate them whenever, for whatever reason, the population faces local pressures.

In effect, Nature has colour-coded their enemies for them so when there is a shortage of a resource (land, minerals, energy or whatever), out comes the racial hatred: an excellent tool for the elite of them to manipulate the main body of the public who can move from amiability to becoming war-like in short order.

As a generality, the different colours have colonised different parts of the globe, which has kept the bulk of populations segregated and vulnerable to suggestions that other colours present a threat, real or imaginary.

We hadn't realised what a blessing being technicolour is until we observed the human race in action. As an aside, during our cultural research, we came across the works of a Jackson Pollack, and we were astounded at how closely he had captured our colour and texture. One in particular, *Blue Poles*, made me feel like I was looking into a mirror.

Another divisive factor is their proliferation of governance models.

It's been aeons since we adopted our system of meritocracy which delivers the best qualified, most experienced leaders of the best character as elected by the best qualified, most experienced voters of the best character. The consequence is that we have had a singularity of purpose which has fuelled our progress such that we are light years ahead of Earth in all aspects of life.

You'd be forgiven for thinking that humans have set out to achieve the opposite effect. On the whole, their world leaders are a sorry bunch of megalomaniacs of great cunning but with little moral compass. Their progress was painfully slow for thousands of years but, admittedly, has sped up over the past 200 years. Their overall standard of living has gradually improved but international tensions have risen in parallel so that the gains are threatened by the potential outbreak of war.

The third major dividing factor is their so-called religions. I cannot draw an easy parallel with our culture as we discarded the need for supernatural beliefs to rationalise our existence so long ago, coming to rely on science which aims to explain our existence, as opposed to religion which confuses. On Earth, the equivalent is called 'humanism' but its adherents rarely appear in the ranks of the elected leaders.

This has, of course, led to major, irrational conflicts with opposite sides frequently claiming the support of the same God or Gods.

Ironically, at its core, all human religions preach the same message of love which governs the behaviour of individuals and small groups as previously observed, but this is fragile and quickly breaks down and ultimately fails on any larger scale.

Our assessment is that the human race is on the road to oblivion, either physically destroying each other or falling victim to a common fate such as the overheating of the planet due to their inability to act in a coordinated manner.

We explained all of this in our last communication and requested permission to intervene in human affairs as a parting gift of salvation. This is directly in conflict with our protocols when visiting other planets and species, but we have never seen a situation as bad as this. We have become quite fond of the inhabitants, despite their failings, and would find it very difficult to leave when we have the power to arrest their decline.

Our first suggestion was to assume management of the planet for a transition period. Using our weapons, we could neutralise them in seconds without them even having time to retaliate. Having a common 'enemy' might distract them from their preoccupation with colour for long enough for the stupidity of it all to dawn on them, particularly when compared to us in all our technicolour glory. We could then install more effective government processes and begin an education programme to wean them off religion. We think this would only take a few hundred years.

A second option was to select one outstanding human and take them into our confidence. We would reveal the secrets of our success and send them out to spread the word to the rest of humanity.

Thirdly, we proposed just giving them one piece of technology: nuclear fission. This would resolve their renewable energy issue and its impact on global warming, giving them time to sort themselves out.

We wonder what reaction we will get.

16th December 2023 Earth Time

This is our final journal entry written as we leave Earth's atmosphere on our long journey home.

Home Base was very pleased with our work and accepted our assessment that Earth was no threat whatsoever to our people.

Our recommendations for current action were noted but rejected. Interim management was regarded as far too radical a step. It was felt that we would get involved in a complicated situation from which we could not withdraw. More pragmatically, the cost of such an operation would be prohibitive, putting undue stress on the budget. So it appears that even an advanced species such as ours is not immune from voter unrest.

With regard to our second option, it was pointed out that there are many Earth precedents of selected humans being provided with enough information to ensure peace on Earth: Moses, Jesus, Mohammed, Buddha, Joseph Smith… It had never ended well with yet another religion spawned to increase the chaos.

Prima facie, a surreptitious gift of nuclear fission may be a good idea but everything we had told them about human civilisation led them to believe that the power would be abused thus perhaps hastening the end.

The matter had been referred to our Supreme Government Council and they had sympathised with us. Whilst being opposed in principle to any interference, they gave us permission to do something really simple in the hope that it would give the humans a steer in the right direction.

During our stay, we had been very careful not to reveal our presence but now the Council has suggested that we do so.

We were to appear before the ironically named United Nations, advise them of our existence, emphasise that we represented no threat and offer our long-term assistance in overcoming their common problems. The rationale being that, if the human race became aware that they were not alone in the Universe, if they saw that the differences between themselves were dwarfed by the differences between them and us, and finally, if we gave them hope that their challenges would be overcome, then they would unite behind the common cause of world peace and prosperity.

We would remind them that the purposes of the UN are 'to maintain international peace and security, develop friendly relations among nations, achieve international cooperation, and serve as a centre for harmonising the actions of nations'.

This we did.

I thought that our presentation went rather well once the UN representatives got over their initial shock. We did have to exercise a certain level of mind control to begin with, but they eventually settled down.

However, as soon as we left the chamber, the old paranoia and uncontrolled aggression emerged. Each of the many sides claimed that this was a power grab by their traditional opposition and within hours, some reckless individual pressed a red button. The nuclear war to end all nuclear wars had begun.

As I update this journal, I am looking out of the porthole watching Earth blow itself apart. We all agree that we are upset about this outcome, but all is not lost.

At least, we will have something by which to remember Earth…

I nicked *Blue Poles*.

PROMOTED AND PROUD

Liz felt like Boadicea returning from the sacking of London as she swung the Jag into the Sainsbury's car park, gliding into the rows of cars assembled like a metallic guard of honour.

It had been a truly victorious day. The Board had unanimously endorsed her promotion and she felt like she ruled the world.

She carried herself with confident authority as she strode towards the supermarket which shone like a fairy-lit castle in the early evening. The automatic doors swished open as if by royal command.

Nick met her at the entrance as he always did on their Thursday night shopping trips. He congratulated her profusely on her promotion and then followed her like a footman as they cruised the aisles. He was an enthusiastic shopper, waxing lyrical about the freshness of the salads and the selection of cheeses. Nick was a lot younger than her and had an exuberance that she would like to have bottled and injected. He could create an entire week's menus in his head as he prowled the aisles, quickly picking the ingredients from the shelves like a conjurer.

Tonight, she noticed the flowers seemed to have been arranged as a tribute to her. The variety of fruit and vegetables was stunning and she imagined the Subjects of the Empire slaving under a hot sun just for her pleasure. She insisted they buy the 'free trade' produce to reward their loyalty and industry.

Each week, they chose the same checkout girl, a sweet young thing called Brenda from Southwark. Nick chatted pleasantly to her while Liz packed the bags.

The news of her promotion to Chair of Sainsbury's had already reached the store and the staff were on high alert, including Brenda. As a regular customer, Brenda already knew who Liz was but was still impressed by the promotion and congratulated her on the same. Liz noted Brenda's new nervousness but understood why she would be feeling overawed. Liz calculated roughly that she was Brenda's ten times boss, at least. She knew she held Brenda's job in her hands and so did Brenda.

It was a very different Liz who visited Sainsbury's to do her shopping on subsequent Thursday nights.

Liz had experienced the absolute high of her career when she was promoted, only to be brought down to earth immediately afterwards when Nick confessed to having an affair. She found it all too irritating and had no alternative but to show him the door. Her pride was at stake here.

In reality, it had not been too much of an inconvenience, except on Thursday nights when he had been a serious asset. The familiar shelves now seemed to scowl at her as if judging her for her lack of imagination. By comparison to the past, Liz's weekly shop was resulting in some very dull meals.

Routinely, she would head towards Brenda's till, comforted to encounter a friendly face after battling the hostile aisles.

Brenda, on the other hand, was becoming less comfortable by the week. She would watch the much-reduced Liz approach with great pity and vowed for the umpteenth time to call off her affair with Nick.

Thursday nights were becoming absolutely intolerable.

THE LAST MINI COOPER

Randle sat in the Horseshoe, staring into his third pint of McLaughlin's, wondering what had hit him. Around him, the crash of crockery marked the end of the luncheon session and sated patrons headed for the street, leaving him alone with his thoughts. His world was falling apart and his gelled, spiky hair seemed to wilt with his mood.

Life as a Hampstead estate agent had been enviable. The work was undemanding to the point of occasional boredom. The pay was great and pulling the birds unchallenging. Hampstead property was always in demand so, historically, it had not been too difficult to make the sales necessary to support his lifestyle. Not that he would want to live in Hampstead himself, of course: he preferred the edgier areas of town, Islington say, where the locals didn't force the closure of every decent nightclub five minutes after it'd opened.

At least, that is what it was like until the property crash of 2008. Now, in June of 2011, the property market and Randle had simultaneously hit rock bottom. He had just received his P45, the last one in his office to do so, and the doors had been depressingly locked behind him.

Over the last few years, one by one, the estate agents had closed shop, in the face of falling demand. Heath Street became a procession of boarded windows. Gone were the attractive advertisements for the village's houses and flats with their lovely, plump prices. Behind them, the attractive, young salesfolk had sat staring blankly at their PC screens, casually feigning productivity until the next punter called. What a loss to the streetscape, Randle thought.

Faced with growing animosity from the local population, the Council had been forced to reduce the rents and small businesses had gradually returned. Randle saw this as a retrograde step as these newcomers – a butcher's and a grocer's, fashion outlets, fish restaurant etc. – were of no interest to him and cruelly reminded him of his departed colleagues. Sadly, the mobile phone outlets went the same way. It was as if their only customers had left town. Faced with well-stocked, queue-less competition, Tesco had been forced out and was now a garden centre. In Randle's mind things had gone seriously downhill.

Grudgingly, he acknowledged that the locals, although faced with a drop in the value of their property, seemed to relish this return to Hampstead past.

He downed his pint and stalked around the corner into Church Row where his garishly decorated, company mini cooper was parked. He loved that car, and the modern, fast life it represented. He had found that he couldn't bear to be parted with it, and had accepted it in lieu of redundancy money. He ripped the parking ticket from the wiper and flung it into the gutter. Slamming the door, he started the engine and roared off down Fitzjohn's Avenue in a cloud of tyre smoke.

Behind him, Hampstead relaxed.

KNIGHT-TIME BLUES

'Arise, Sir Richard.'

My heart is sinking, but my body rises as ordered by Her Majesty.

The Queen glances in the direction of my wife and teenage daughter, whose naive eyes are moist with pride. They are in the front row of the audience in the ornate Buckingham Palace Ballroom and are leaning forward with anticipation. They are behind me now, but I spotted them as I was being announced by the Lord Chamberlain. If the Queen has identified them as my kin, then I find this very impressive, but I suppose a thousand investitures have made her acutely sensitive to the tell-tale signs of personal involvement. I can't be sure, of course. Maybe one of them has simply dropped a glove.

Despite my depression, I feel a reciprocated sense of pride in them. They are both attractive women and don't look out of place in these splendid surroundings, an effect achieved at my own considerable expense in the boutiques of Knightsbridge. The careful, neutral tones of their outfits blend in well with the rich red carpet and furnishings, and their diamond jewellery flickers in the light of the crystal chandeliers. Because I exclude them from my business dealings, they don't realise that I am going through this charade for their benefit only, as *I* wouldn't give tuppence for a knighthood. Well, more accurately, I'd probably give you half a million pounds – which I believe is the going rate – but this one has cost me a lot more than that.

I wonder what the Queen is thinking at a time like this. Does she know who I am and what I do? Would she be shocked to learn that she has just honoured a property developer, pariah of the human race, exploiter of the poor and weak? I hope not, as she may think that she can put her sword to better use by decapitating me. From here, it's certainly hard to tell what's going on in her mind. She has the inscrutable countenance of a discreet basset hound.

Mind you, the Royals are no strangers to the property market. Young Charlie seems intent on covering the south of England with mock-Georgian villages and certainly doesn't allow objectors to stand in his way, so it would be hypocritical for her to feel superior, at least on that score anyway; on unearned inherited power and wealth she'd win hands down.

I've heard that the profligate and cash-strapped George IV came up with a scheme to raise funds by developing Regent's Park but was deterred when his Prime Minister advised him of the potential cost – *two crowns*. George would understand my current feelings.

'Well done, Sir Richard. We are very impressed by your clever efforts and you justly deserve your reward.' *Hmm?*

'Thank you, Ma'am. I am very honoured,' I reply with becoming humility.

'Apart from your philanthropic works, I believe that you are a property developer?'

'That's correct, Your Majesty, but only in a small way in the Hampstead area.'

'What a lovely part of the world. We do like Hampstead and have old friends with property there. Is this a good area for investment?'

'Well, to be honest, things have been better.'

'Oh, dear. Well, we wish you every good fortune in your future dealings.'

'Thank you, Ma'am.'

Well, at least, she knows who and what I am. Her equerry must have briefed her earlier as I made my long journey to the investiture kneeling stool, nervous that I would perform an involuntary somersault in front of three hundred people. Conscious that I am holding up the queue of waiting worthies,

I now back away, head bowed, to collect my insignia and join my overawed relatives. On the high balcony behind us, the Household Military Band plays gently, inducing me into a trance-like state of relief and disbelief.

What a weird turn of events.

There is a theory that most world events occur as the unintended consequences of decisions taken for other reasons. An example is London's dominance in capital markets, a result of the US government's attempt to punish the USSR during the Cold War by forbidding American banks from loaning it money, thus leaving the way clear for the British banks to gain the advantage.

I wouldn't say my situation is on such an important scale, but the last thing I expected when I started my little scheme was to end up here in Buck House meeting Queenie.

If anyone is to blame for my predicament, it is the late Peter Cook, comedian and infamous Hampstead resident. I never met the man but I used to see him occasionally around the village, lugubriously scanning the morning papers in the 'Coffee Cup' on the High Street. He was a great practical joker and one of his pranks was my inspiration. He started a tongue-in-cheek campaign to build a golf course with attendant resort on Hampstead Heath, causing outrage.

It has to be remembered that Hampstead Heath was originally saved from the clutches of Sir Thomas Maryon-Wilson, Lord of the Manor and property developer (gasp!) in the mid-1800s by a nationwide, public protest which spawned the Heath and Hampstead Society, the world's first conservation association.

So Peter was poking in a very sensitive area, as he well knew.

Meanwhile, the Queen is doing a good job of processing this procession of admirable citizens, and my two companions are enthralled. She takes about a minute with each individual and gives the appearance of being genuinely interested in them all. This is some skill, given that there are so many of us, but not a skill valued in my own harsh, professional world where showing personal respect is a sign of weakness.

Five members of the Queen's Bodyguard are keeping a watchful eye on proceedings and I could certainly have used their services to gain some respect on one or two difficult occasions in the past.

I remember being highly amused by Cook's idea and the public reaction to it. At the time, I was quite interested in golf and had been taking lessons so I could join a club. I was able therefore to imagine the proposed course layout and my developer's mind could calculate the huge theoretical financial gains.

Once my swing was honed, I applied for membership of the Hampstead Golf Club and to my horror, was declined. They gave me no reason, but I suspect that my profession was the stumbling block. It was while I was reading the rejection letter that the BIG IDEA came to me. I decided that I would adapt Peter Cook's proposal to suit my purposes. By whatever means, I would gain control of the golf club site, convert it into a luxury housing estate and pocket millions. If I couldn't play golf on the damn course, nobody would. Not all that philanthropic a motive, I'm afraid, Your Majesty.

Successful members of my trade use an age-old recipe of skills: subterfuge, treachery and misrepresentation, mixed together with lashings of insincerity and duplicitous diplomacy and we are proud of it. Without our contribution the country, and specifically Hampstead, would stagnate. How would the burgeoning population be accommodated without new houses, flats, in-fills and conversions? People would be forced to live miles from their place of employment, at great cost to their financial and social welfare. In my view, the end justifies the means, a credo observed by the predecessors of the

Illustrious Personage performing her duties in front of me now. Henry VIII, for instance. Enough said.

I realised that this project would require all of these skills, employed to perfection.

Hampstead has a long history of thwarting development, so it would be a tough assignment. Take poor old Sir Thomas for instance. His family had owned land on Hampstead Heath for centuries but when he decided to develop it for housing, he ran into a brick-wall of opposition. He fought bitterly for forty years (appropriately building his own brickworks on the Heath), and only his death brought an end to the battle.

His heirs capitulated and sold the Heath into public ownership for the market price (some capitulation), developed their newly inherited, extensive landholdings between Hampstead and Kilburn without opposition, and made a fortune. Their descendants are still happily and quietly collecting the ground rents for most of the borough, thank you very much.

Within this historical context and given the aggression of the Heath and Hampstead Society, the enterprise would need a degree of deviousness beyond anything I had achieved previously, but hurt pride fuelled my imagination. The trick was to find a way of presenting the plan as being in the community's interest and harnessing the general distaste for golf clubs (seen as elitist), and golf courses (regarded as a waste of space).

Last year, an eleven-acre property bordering the Heath sold for £40 million, and there was no shortage of bidders. So I knew that there was market demand, and here were forty acres of prime real estate being used for the pleasure of a privileged few. I figured that I could get a million pounds an acre if I could pull it all off.

Stage 1 of my plan was to initiate a propaganda campaign against Hampstead Golf Club. This was done anonymously and by cashing in some old favours with the press. Over the succeeding months, a series of revelations filled the tabloids. The accusations of racism, elitism, sexism, homophobia and pollution, not to mention paedophilia, bestiality and impoliteness to old ladies caused a great stir and led to angry demonstrations at the club's entrance gates.

With the opposition reduced to its knees, the time was right for Stage 2.

I launched a campaign to reclaim the land for development as a low-cost housing estate and, in a grand altruistic gesture, offered to fund the purchase. In fact, the money would come from my secret backer, a Russian oligarch, on the understanding that, once we had our hands on the property and had secured planning permission, we would switch to developing four ten-acre blocks for sale to his immigrant colleagues.

My close connections at Camden Council assured me that they 'foresaw no difficulties' with this process, just as they 'foresaw no difficulties' in receiving generous contributions to their retirement funds.

These tactics proved to be very successful – way too successful in fact.

The matter attracted national attention and, before I knew it, had become a cause as celebrated as that which saved the blessed Heath in the first place.

Our local Member of Parliament, a former actress, famed for her portrayal of our current queen's like-named ancestor, recognised that this was an opportunity to make some serious political capital, brushed me aside imperiously and took charge.

Before you could say 'Oscar', the government had seized the land by compulsory purchase order and was using the project as evidence of its commitment to getting young, single-parent, underprivileged, first-time buyers on the property ladder.

These unfortunate developments left me with one disgruntled Russian oligarch and a small number of disenchanted Camden officials whose retirement had been delayed by a few years. The former was more a cause for concern than the latter: unhappy oligarchs tending to be more vicious than council officers, although there may not be much in it.

But then the unexpected happened.

Even after I was trumped by the politicians, I had remained in the spotlight and was given credit for the social good which flowed from the campaign. I was the hero of the young, single-parent, disadvantaged, first-time buyers and their parents who were glad to see the back of them.

Ironically, I was now the most popular man in the Village. I had never experienced such public esteem, being more used to vilification for my profiteering ways.

What started as local acclaim became national. I was perceived as a modern miracle, a convert from the evil world of capitalism to the true path of socialism. Someone, somewhere in Whitehall decided that I should be set up as an example and, to my utter amazement, I was awarded this knighthood.

In no way does this compensate me for the lost millions, but it has served to get my oligarchic friend off my back, as he sees some advantage in having a titled associate to sit on the boards of his various companies, conferring upon them an undeserved air of respectability.

These are the events that have led me to be sitting here, a little bemused, a little sad, watching Elizabeth the Second deal with the tail end of the honoured few as the band plays on.

She finishes doling out the final, miserly MBEs (not worth more than £5,000), has a quiet word with her equerry and trots off to perform other important regal acts, grooming corgis no doubt.

The show being over, my devoted wife and daughter offer extravagant hugs and we make our way towards the exit.

I understand that it is customary for the recently elevated to lunch at the Ritz, after a self-satisfied stroll through Green Park. Each of us is limited to three guests at the ceremony, so if one wants to impress on a grander scale, then lunch at the Ritz is the answer. I imagine the wine and compliments will flow in equal volume for the rest of the afternoon and into the evening.

Much to my two companions' disappointment, I have no stomach for such celebrations, and decide to head back up to Hampstead. The lost millions weigh too heavily on my mind.

'Excuse me, Sir Richard, may I have a quick word?'

It's the Queen's equerry. He's taken me entirely by surprise, particularly with the form of address he employed. This 'Sir Richard' business is growing on me.

My wife and daughter discreetly withdraw, leaving me alone with Commander Laurence Timmons, as he introduces himself.

'The Queen is very interested in your background, Sir Richard. We at the Palace have been doing our research and we think that a man of your talents might just be of assistance to Her Majesty.'

'Naturally, I would be honoured to help in whatever way I can, but I fail to understand how that might be.'

'Now, I am going to take you into my confidence here and we expect complete discretion. You will be aware of the growing public debate about the cost of the monarchy and the scrutiny being applied to all aspects of royal income and expenditure. Since 1993, the Queen has been paying tax on her personal income and she is finding the cost of supporting her extended, rather extravagant family becoming more and more of a burden. Recently, when the Queen refused to foot his nuptial bill, her grandson sold the photographic rights to *Hello!* magazine. This has embarrassed us into action.'

'Fair enough, Commander, but what can I do?'

'The Queen has an extensive property portfolio, but is unable to maximise profits because of numerous legal and political constraints. We need someone to take, let's say, a more "imaginative" view and to devise less conventional ways for its exploitation. Our informants tell us that you may be our man. I hasten to add that we are contemplating a "partnership" style of relationship here, so the rewards could be quite considerable.'

'And who might those informants be?'

'The Maryon-Wilson family. You may have come across them?'

'Yes, indeed. It's always a pleasure to deal with professionals. Are you fixed for lunch, Commander? Perhaps you'd like to join my family and me at the Ritz?'

Why You?

Why have they sent you, little girl,
with your camera and questions?
The Yard's no place for womenfolk
with sad, unsettling faces.

For thirty years, we've worked our shifts,
outfitting the ships for sea,
so we've really nothing left to learn
from modern lassies, running free.

So on your bike and out the gate
with your rumours and your lies,
before the foreman spies you.
Ah, but one last thing before you go:

What is this 'asbestosis'?

SUPERPOWER SYNDROME

'Good morning, Ms Danvers, or may I call you "Kara", or even "Supergirl"?'

'Morning, Doctor. "Ms Danvers" will do fine. I only exposed my secret identity to my GP when he was having difficulty giving me a kryptonite inoculation, so I would prefer to keep that confidential, if you don't mind?'

'No problem at all. "Ms Danvers", it is. Would you prefer the chair or the couch? Whichever makes you most comfortable.'

'I'll take the chair, thank you.'

'Now Ms Danvers, your GP has referred you to me regarding some emotional issues you are experiencing but he's non-specific, saying you'd prefer to explain in person. I'm sure I will be able to help but perhaps we could start by your describing the symptoms? Take your time.'

'With respect, I'd like to do a reference check first. Why are you so confident you can sort things out for me? We superheroes have special needs and need special treatment, after all.'

'Well, Ms Danvers, I've dealt successfully with a number of your colleagues with mental health issues. Not that I'm saying you have a mental health issue, of course. The side effects of being a superhero, "Super Power Syndrome" as I call it, can be quite debilitating without the sufferer being certifiably insane. For instance, your cousin Superman came to see me suffering from lack of sleep due to his X-ray vision. I prescribed a lead sleeping mask. Problem solved.'

'It would reassure me if you would share some more case studies with me.'

'Not a problem. Of course, I will need to protect the privacy of my patients but you are "one of the gang" so to speak, and you know how to keep a secret. Let's see where to begin? Well, last year I treated Spiderman.'

'What was his problem?'

'Arachnophobia.'

'Get away! How does that work?'

'Young Parker was absolutely petrified by his alter ego. Remember, it all started when he was bitten by one of the little blighters. A perfectly understandable reaction, I would say.'

'So how did you treat him?'

'With great ingenuity.'

'Some detail, please.'

'It was a matter of proving to Parker that Spiderman was no threat to him and I did this by exposing him to inky dinky little spiders and working up to tarantulas. Then I had him sit through all the Spiderman movies while feeding him chocolate and soft drinks to create a positive experience. Worked a treat.'

'I'm glad to hear that. And Peter is back to normal?'

'Parker certainly is but here's a complication. An unintentional consequence, if you will.'

'What's that?'

'Spiderman is now suffering from anthropophobia.'

'What on earth is that?'

'Fear of humans. Not sure yet what I'm going to do about that. I can't use the same tactics as it's virtually impossible to find a person in this modern world who isn't at least a bit scary but never mind, I'll work it out.'

'That's not all that encouraging. Who else is there?'

'Well, there's Dr Robert Banner aka The Hulk. I treated Banner for anger management. This proved so successful that The Hulk virtually disappeared. Nearly killed off the series. Stan Lee was beside himself and gave me a fortune to reverse the process. I offered to treat Stan for anger management as well, which really set him off.'

'Where has this been left?'

'As compensation for the loss of a client, Stan is paying me to work with The Hulk. He's not all that easy to communicate with and he's a little volatile. I'm giving him my assertiveness training.'

'Assertiveness? The Hulk? You have to be joking?'

'He's quite shy when you get to know him.'

'This isn't getting any better. Who else?'

'I don't think we want to go near Batman and Robin, do we?'

'That's gross and that's enough. Against my better judgement, let's move onto my problem.'

'Sure, what can I help you with?'

'Fear of flying.'

'Too obvious.'

'Yes, you're right. Too obvious. It's a man thing. I've got a crush on Jimmy Olsen and he pays me absolutely no attention. It's driving me insane.'

'Oh, heavy duty stuff then. This is more teenage angst than Super Power Syndrome. Have you considered just growing up, Supergirl? Maybe delete "girl", insert "woman"?'

'OK, I'll generalise the problem if you'll take me more seriously. I'm having trouble forming a physical relationship with the opposite sex.'

'I don't find that altogether surprising. Looking at this rationally, you have to accept that you are, by definition, an alien so we are talking about interspecies sex. Down here we have a term for it, "bestiality" and it's illegal so you might expect our males to be a little standoffish. No offence meant.'

'Offence most certainly taken. I'm sure that this hasn't been a factor. Superman and Lois Lane seemed to manage OK.'

'That's true. Although I have never been sure what, if anything, ever happened between them. Have you talked to him about this?'

'No, we don't have that sort of relationship.'

'Have you thought of trying it on with Superman? It's OK between cousins and gets rid of the interspecies complication.'

'Oh, yuk.'

'Just a suggestion. Thinking about it, there are other considerations at play. Your super powers would be daunting. Not that being "stronger than a locomotive" is as impressive as it once was. Mind you, you could still crush a man to death in a fit of passion which might put a few off. After all, self-preservation is a powerful motive.'

'And your ability to fly eliminates all possibility of the guy getting to drive. There are masculine self-respect issues around this. Not to mention the threat to privacy of your X-ray vision. Look I'm really not sure if I can be of much help to you with this problem.'

'Hey, I thought I'd get some sympathy from a female psychiatrist.'

'You thought wrong, Ms Danvers. Also, don't you think you're being a little selfish about this?'

'How do you mean?'

'Haven't you considered the effect you and Superman have had on humanity? We've spent millions of years getting to the top of the evolutionary tree and you come along and knock us back to ground level. Why do you think the Olympics have been cancelled? Running the hundred metres in under ten seconds is now pathetic. You've made the high jump redundant and our puny attempts at the discus and shotput are meaningless. You've made us all feel totally inadequate. Perhaps this explains our males' lack of attraction? I suggest that you buy yourself a cat and get over it.

'That will be a thousand dollars, Ms Danvers. Please pay on the way out.'

REFLECTIVE

'Will this do you, Joe?' asked Helen hesitantly as she wheeled him under the chestnut tree out of the sun.

She could tell that he had been a big man by the size of his hands and feet and she knew from the records that he'd had a hard life. He was a man who said very little, a loner. Although he was old now, he still radiated a sense of malice.

Wisely, she kept her distance.

'Yep,' grunted Joe as he adjusted his blanket impatiently over his grey trousers. With no interest he watched her trim, uniformed figure depart. *There's no such thing as a good woman.* Joe had a conviction born of experience.

As far as Joe enjoyed anything, he liked it out here in the grounds where they parked him on fine summer mornings out of the way. The open fields gave him space to breathe and he drew comfort from the size and strength of the protective chestnut.

Except on days like today, he had no contact with living things, other than the odd, unwelcome human.

Every now and then he would reach out and stroke the tree's rough surface as if seeking reassurance that there was still something alive and benign in his otherwise hostile world.

Another small pleasure for him was the absence of walls. Sure there were enclosing fences but they were well out of the range of Joe's aged eyesight. There had been so many walls in his life that the horizon had always been a novelty to him.

'Now, I'm too bloody blind to see it,' he complained to the thin air.

He calculated how many walls he'd stared at in his time and for how many hours. This took a while but eventually he guessed it to be a thousand walls and a quarter of a million hours.

'Jeez, that's depressing. Just more measures of a wasted life,' he said to the tree as if speaking to a sympathetic friend.

'At least out here, I'm clocking up my "free" time. Not that I can do much with it in my clapped-out state.'

But it was the absence of people that was the best thing.

He couldn't think of a single relationship he'd had with another human being that had not ended up causing him grief. Even his parents had resented his presence and could not disguise their relief when he left home as a snarling teenager.

Then there was the disaster of his marriage to Sue. It was the only love he'd known but it had turned sour eventually. He'd done his best to provide for her and the brats in the only way he knew how but all she'd ever done was to complain.

After his arrest, she'd done a bunk and he hadn't even bothered to try to find her when he'd served that first of many sentences.

'Good riddance,' he thought bitterly, touching the tree as gently as he would Sue, given another chance.

Sculpture by Richard Meier*

Darling, I don't wish to hurt your feelings
but this has to be the worst anniversary present ever
You need to take it back to the dealer

It should be owned by someone who understands
and appreciates art and that's not me
Someone I probably wouldn't like

Sure, you love me
and it cost you a fortune
but it looks like scrap metal
in fact, it is scrap metal

Whatever happened to gold
diamonds and pearls
As expressions of love

Richard Meier's hopeful label, 'Sculpture'
is no help
It's still junk

Do we have to work it out for ourselves?

Meier's buildings are triumphs of design and engineering
All gleaming white and shout out optimism
His sculptures are dark, misshapen and gloomy

I understand buildings
I like buildings
You should have bought one of his buildings
I'd accept with gratitude

I've been looking at this object for long enough now
I can start to see shapes emerging. You really can't help it

It's possible to see two figures, engaging in some way

They might be Greek gods
Perhaps Hephaestus, god of metalworking and his wife
Aphrodite, goddess of love
Offering a love token to prevent her from straying
which she was prone to do on occasion

I'm beginning to see the sculpture in a more favourable light
You said it cost you a fortune. How much?
That much? That's impressive
Hmm? Well, OK, I'll keep it on one condition

… you give it a coat of white paint to brighten it up

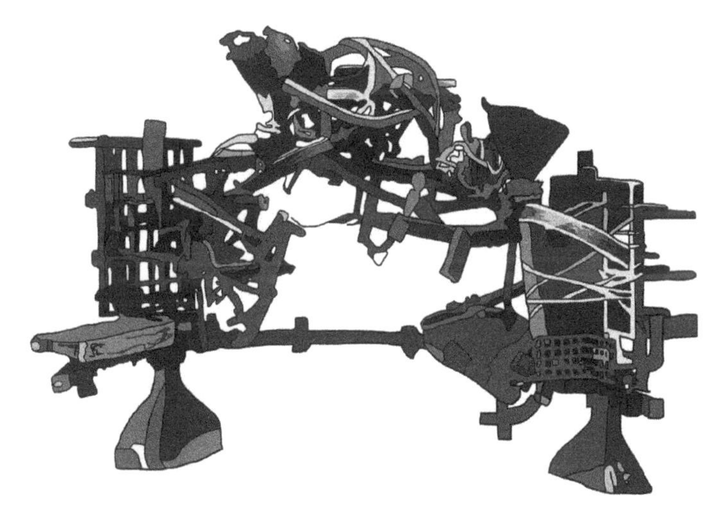

*Sculpture

Richard Meier (b.1934). American architect known for his rationalist designs and the use of the colour white.

THE TABLETS

M: Hi, I wonder if you could give me something for a slightly embarrassing condition?

G: Do you have a prescription?

M: No, I was hoping for something 'over the counter'

G: We'll see what we can do. What are the symptoms?

M: General depression. Lack of purpose. Feeling lost.

G: How long has this been going on?

M: I'd say most of my conscious life.

G: As it happens, I can prescribe some tablets for that but I should warn you, once you take them, you are on them for life.

M: I can handle that.

G: The curious thing about this treatment is that following the instructions is more important than the tablets themselves. In fact, you can lose the tablets and still get relief.

M: Now that's weird but you're the expert. How much do I owe you?

G: We have a special offer on at the moment. In return for making a lifelong, loyalty commitment, you can have them for free.

M: Wow, that sounds like a seriously good deal although, in my experience, these things can turn out rather badly in the long term. But having said that, things are a bit tight at the moment so hand them over.

G: I'll wrap them for you. Will you need a hand carrying them?

M: No, I should be OK. It's all downhill.

G: OK. Well, safe travels, Moses.

M: No worries. Bye G.

VIRTUAL REALTY

Rod and Clare were in their mid-thirties, married for seven years. Rod's career as an auditor had somewhat stalled and his salary had plateaued but Clare was thriving as CEO of a finance company. The mortgage was coming down and all was right in the world.

Except for one thing. They couldn't agree on where to live.

Clare was very content in their small bungalow in semi-rural England. Her parents were nearby and she loved the sense of space. But Rod was a city boy who craved an urban environment where there were restaurants and pubs, not to mention a handy train to save two hours of commute a day.

This was the only topic they argued about and it was making them both very unhappy but neither of them was prepared to compromise. This all came to a head one Friday evening with them ending up sleeping in different bedrooms and not on speaking terms.

Rod was a keen but poor golfer and the next morning he had a terrible round with his concentration straying worse than his drives. This performance was watched with growing anxiety by his playing partners. His dispute with Clare was his one topic of conversation and he'd been boring them to death with it for months. After this round, he would be intolerable when they were trying to relax over a couple of beers.

In anticipation and out of desperation, they had arranged for Gary, a fellow member and local property developer, to join them in the clubhouse in the hope that he might be able to give Rod some advice and give them some peace.

As it happens, Rod knew Gary quite well and, as Gary was a single-figure golfer, Rod was more than slightly in awe of him. Low handicappers' opinions were to be respected in all matters in Rod's mind.

The trick worked and Rod and Gary took themselves off for a private chat, allowing the others to indulge themselves in a meaningless, stroke-by-stroke analysis of the previous five hours, an act which bored them just as much as Rod did but in a warm, safe way.

Gary explained that his company specialised in a new form of property market, called Virtual Realty. This was more of a communal than an individual ownership model. 'Taking the "I" out of "Reality",' he joked.

The deal would be that Rod and Clare would sell their existing property to Gary and in return, Gary would provide them with virtual real estate. They would be totally free to design their property with no constraints. It could be a penthouse or a castle with no limits on the grandeur of the interior decoration. The contract would permit a total redesign every five years at no extra cost.

'It's all in the software,' Gary explained.

To resolve their particular problem, they could have separate external environments. Clare could stay in the country so, when she stepped out of the door, she would be surrounded by green fields and cattle. On the other hand, Rod could live in the centre of any city he desired. He punned that they would be getting 'the best of two worlds'.

Gary then went into a detailed explanation about the scientific principles upon which the scheme was based but it was way above Rod's head and anyway he was already preparing his pitch to Clare.

Gary had put together a detailed proposal for Rod and Clare to consider and handed it over in a glossy folder.

'By the way,' Gary said, 'if it's any comfort to you, I've invested in Virtual Realty myself. One of the reasons is that it's enabled me to keep my handicap so low. The same would be true for you, of course.'

This was the clincher for Rod. He desperately wanted his opinions respected, even if only on the golf course. All he had to do was to get Clare to agree. Too easy.

As Gary handed over the proposal, the light caught the company strapline written in small print: 'The Matrix, Imagine the Home of Your Dream'. As it turned out, Rod was as poor a negotiator as he was a golfer and even the charm and wit of Gary couldn't convince Clare. So they went their separate ways.

Clare now really breeds alpacas and Rod is virtually club champion.

LOANS

TAKING THE TABLETS

'Oh, My God!' exclaimed Moses, but rapidly withdrew the plea.

The last thing he needed was another Visitation. Smoke was stinging his eyes and burning his throat and explosions deafened him as he struggled up Mt Sinai. Ever since the Voice from the burning bush implored him to lead the Lord's people out of Egypt, Moses' life had taken a definite turn for the worse.

As soon as they had set out for the Promised Land, the crowd began to grumble; first it was the threat of the pursuing Egyptians and then lack of water and food. Each time, Moses called for the Lord's help and the Lord obliged. He parted the waters of the Red Sea, let the Israelites through, unsportingly removed the wheels from the Egyptians' chariots, and drowned the lot. The Lord showed him how to make a spring and made manna rain from heaven. Each time the Lord demanded respect from the people in return and each time it was offered all too briefly. A recipe for conflict indeed and Moses found himself caught in the middle.

The last episode had been the worst. God had summoned him up Mt Sinai to receive the Commandments. Moses spent forty days and forty nights in the Lord's company with him endlessly complaining about the seven tribes' conduct. It was very tedious. Just as the time approached to go back down for some peace, God discovered that the Israelites were worshipping a golden calf. This set him off again. Moses stormed down the mountain, smashed the Commandments in anger, and berated the mob, before turning resignedly to scale the mountain again.

Spluttering and with his ears ringing, Moses stumbled out of the smoke into a vast clearing. Everything went suddenly quiet and the air was filled with the scent of cherry blossoms, leaving

Moses temporarily stunned. As he regained his senses, he took stock of his surroundings. In front of him, stood a building, several times the size of Cheops's pyramid. Mesmerised, he wandered towards the massive front portal and stopped in astonishment when he noticed a waiting queue, comprised of weird beings, even more fantastic than the Egyptian gods.

Suddenly, a hand planted itself on his shoulder and he jumped several cubits into the air. Spinning around, he came face-to-stomach with an Angel. He would never get used to the size of God's messengers and it was even worse when they spread their wings as this one was doing. Moses dropped to his knees in supplication but the Angel reached down and gently lifted him to his feet.

'Where am I?' cowered Moses, 'and who are you?'

'Welcome to the Milky Way Branch of the Lord's Library. I am his Chief Librarian, at your service. I can see this is something of a shock for you, Moses, but all is well. God has got into a huff over the idol thing and flounced off to another galaxy. Don't worry, he'll get over it; he always does. You're here to collect a replacement set of tablets, I believe.'

The Librarian explained that the library held a set of commandments for every society in the Universe, with each set unique. The occupants of the queue, who had so startled Moses, were prophets from every corner of the Universe and from every period of history, waiting to collect God's instructions.

'Do you realise that you can define a society if you know what its ten worst sins are? For instance, your lot are not allowed to covet your neighbour's ass which places you in a time and place where asses are valuable. This wouldn't be appropriate in twentieth-century New York, or any time at all on Mars.'

'New York, Mars?' asked Moses blankly as he struggled to come to grips with the fact that God was more liberal with his affections than he had been led to believe.

'Oh, never mind,' said the Librarian. 'Let's find your tablets before you have a breakdown.'

He led Moses by the hand to the head of the queue, ignoring the complaints of those who had been waiting patiently for hours. For some of them, lunch was long overdue, and they were having difficulty resisting the temptation to eat their neighbour thus violating their Eighth Commandment.

Once they had located the replacement tablets, the Librarian escorted Moses back to the edge of the plateau and bid him farewell.

'So Moses, now what are you going to tell the Chosen People?'

'I'll tell them that the Almighty has given them a set of commandments they deserve; in that sense, they are chosen.'

There goes a worthy prophet indeed thought the Librarian. *May he be recognised in his own land.*

THE SCENT OF SUCCESS

Most superheroes gain their powers by virtue of some cataclysmic event such as an explosion during a laboratory experiment, an insect bite or a risky escape from a planet at war. In my case, I did it the boring way, by going to the SuperHero college, the Avengers Academy.

Virtually no one knows of its existence as they keep a very low profile and attendance is by invitation only. Tuition is free and the college is funded by the Marvel superheroes, The Avengers, some of whom are alumni. The likes of The Hulk and Iron Man have made a fortune from their movies and public appearances and they like to put something back, in addition to conquering evil.

The Academy is highly discriminating about who they let in. As far as I can judge, they select the mildest personalities and frailest of physiques. Presumably, this is to heighten the contrast between before and after the granting of superpowers. This makes for good cinema and it should be remembered where the funding ultimately comes from.

So, the unexpected letter of offer is not actually the most flattering of life's surprises, although one doesn't realise that at the time. I admit that, at first, I thought it was a hoax and I took some convincing that such an institution existed and that the invitation was for real.

My equally sceptical parents took me to an interview with the Academy Principal, who went by the title of Head. This turned out to be seriously appropriate as he was, in fact, a disembodied, floating head which we all found a little disconcerting. After a while, we got used to him and put aside some of the biological questions raised by a being inconveniently missing most of its body parts.

The Head explained that it was a three-year SuperHero degree course aimed at preparing students for life as a SuperHero. It was purely theoretical in nature as we were not yet trusted with any powers. The topics ranged from 'Techniques for Time and Space

Travel', through 'The Faults in Einstein's Theory of Relativity and Their Exploitation for the Benefit of Humankind' to 'Successful Auditioning'. There was a lot of emphasis placed on the ethics involved in using one's powers as I was led to believe that they'd had a few problems over time with SuperHeroes going rogue.

Once you graduated you were given your power and embarked on a one-year Masters of the Universe Diploma. Then you were let loose to fight evil in all its forms, to make the odd movie and to open supermarkets. Unfortunately, the growth in online shopping had reduced opportunities in this latter category, driving the SuperHeroes to augment their income with after-dinner speaking engagements, something at which they were notoriously bad due to SuperHeroes not typically possessing the necessary sense of humour or irony. The Head told us that they were including coaching in this in the next semester's curriculum. We found this reassuring.

In my mild-mannered way, I did well and, in the fullness of time, I graduated with honours. My parents proudly attended the graduation ceremony when I would receive my superpower. A few Avengers were there, although none of them were invited to speak.

The graduates did not know what power they might be given and our imaginations ran riot. Would we have the strength and endurance of Captain America and be equipped with an indestructible Vibranium shield? I imagined myself as Hawkeye, he of the unerring accuracy as a bowman and the sharpest of wits.

We were called one at a time in alphabetical order to the dais to learn our fate from the Head. The students are each given a different power, so being early in the queue is preferable. It is at times like these that I resent the fact that my name, Zimmerman, puts me at such a disadvantage. I made a note to change my name to Ackerman when this was all over.

I watched as each of my classmates was handed an envelope which they fumbled to open, before reading the contents to an excited audience. (It wasn't until afterwards that I questioned how the Head 'handed' out the envelopes. It's a mystery.) My heart sank as the best powers were endowed upon others. Bill Earnshaw flew from the stage and Betty Robinson displayed her X-ray vision by revealing the contents of her mother's handbag, much to her mother's embarrassment. But hey, what could she expect if she's going to bring that sort of equipment to a gathering of decent folk?

Eventually, my turn came and the Head handed me the last envelope. My brain went into autopilot and I opened and blurted out the contents without processing it. There was an audible gasp from the crowd when I said 'Super Sense of Smell'.

Gradually, the import of this penetrated the emotional fog which enveloped my mind. I was being sent out into the world to fight the bad guys, armed only with an acute sense of smell.

My disappointment must have been clear to all present and the Head, taking pity on me, drew an envelope from somewhere and tenderly proffered it to me. Again, I opened and read it without thinking. There was an even louder reaction from the auditorium when I announced 'Super Pedantry'.

Presumably, I was to sniff out wrong doers and then bore them to death.

I immediately thought of Superman and his catchphrase: 'This is a job for Superman. Up, up and away!'

Mine would be 'This is a Super Nose job. Book me an Uber.' Doesn't quite have the same ring.

Those Avengers present gathered around me to offer their condolences. With my new powers, I remember wishing that they would stand a bit further away. Fighting crime makes you fusty.

In any event, they cooked up a plan by which I could put my talents to best use and this is how I came to be appointed as the

Secretary of the Avengers Board of Directors. They figured the meetings would be on time and the minutes accurate.

This was a great experience and great fun. To see my heroes up close was a privilege and to hear of their exploits was educational.

During these meetings, a story emerged of a particularly elusive villain, called 'Interfero'. He was so named because he roamed the universe interfering in elections, causing mayhem, unrest and even wars. He had the ability to shape change in both a physical and policy sense. He would become indistinguishable from the local population, assume leadership of one of the mainstream parties and begin espousing populist policies aimed at confusion and destabilisation. He would switch policies at whim, often suddenly adopting the polar opposite position without embarrassment and without losing the support of his adulating base. Once he had done enough damage he moved on. No one knew why he did this, other than perhaps out of ego.

The Avengers had been trying to neutralise him for decades but each time, before they became aware of his activities, he had disappeared. The only evidence they had of his existence was a simple pink comb that he had dropped at a rally. It came with a few strands of blond hair which they had used for DNA testing, but he turned out to be of no known life form.

As I sat there taking the minutes, I was aware of the significant frustration in the room. Thor was so agitated that he kept smashing furniture.

And then it dawned on me. With my super sense of smell, maybe I could find him?

'Give me a spacecraft and I will find Interfero for you!' I said dramatically.

All heads turned towards me with astonishment. I think they'd forgotten I was there.

'What have we got to lose?' said Captain America.

The next day I arrived at his last sighting place, a smoking, ruined planet, and using the comb to get his scent, began to track him down. We zigzagged from galaxy to galaxy, diving down wormholes and warping from dimension to dimension. Such was my power that I could detect him even through the ship's blast shields and across the vast vacuum of space.

And we found him. . . at 721-725 Fifth Avenue, New York. Admittedly, the name of the building was a bit of a giveaway, Interfero Tower.

My superhero friends quickly arrested him and he was brought before the Intergalactic Court of Justice. I was appointed the Chief Prosecutor and, using my power of pedantry, delivered an opening address of such minute detail with such polished public speaking style, that Interfero was on his knees pleading guilty within a matter of months. Even the judge was begging for mercy as she lay quivering beneath her bench.

Interfero was sentenced to home confinement for life under my supervision. His appeal to have this reduced to the death penalty was denied.

This was a godsend for me as I appointed him to the position of assistant Secretary of the Avengers Board and this freed me up to take part in the business discussions. Modestly, I like to think that I improved the quality of the debate with my command of the facts, and eloquence. Unfortunately, a sudden increase in the crime rate meant that attendance at the Board dropped sharply and we have had to cancel most of the meetings.

Now I spend my time educating Interfero on the finer aspects of wine appreciation, using my enhanced sense of smell. He doesn't say much but I can tell he enjoys these sessions as much as I do by the glint in his eye.

Life is good.

STRANGER ON THE CANAL

Chantal watched Raymond walk away with regret.

They had only known each other for one week but her mind was overwhelmed by new memories and emotions. He moved with grace and looked unconsciously comfortable in his simple, dark clothes. Turning at the top of the steps into Carcassonne Station, he waved briefly and eased out of sight. Compared to the person she had first met, he cut a more confident figure and she had to resist a strong urge to run after him.

As she drove her battered red van back to the Canal du Midi and the *Clair de Lune*, she recalled how he had materialised magically last Saturday at the side of the canal in the evening mist. Chantal and her three fellow crew members were busy preparing the boat for his arrival and were alerted to his presence by a sudden, and highly unusual, burst of birdsong.

The boat's owner, Serge, had asked them to stay an extra week after the season's end to do one last trip up the canal. He had agreed to do a favour for an old school friend, Raymond, whose father had died and who needed a quiet period to compose himself before inheriting his new responsibilities. Although he stopped short of explaining these, Serge left the impression that they were onerous.

This request was unprecedented. The *Clair de Lune* was purpose-built to take up to six passengers and it was not economical to take a single guest. Also, as skipper, Jean-Paul, who had over twenty years' experience on the canal protested, all the locks would be closed until the spring. Serge assured him that arrangements had been made and all would be well. The barge's chef, Yves, complained when he learnt that the mystery traveller was a vegetarian and the hostess, Anna from Manchester, grumbled at the prospect of delaying her reunion with her boyfriend and dog after six weeks' continuous cruising. Serge offered them generous compensation which settled the matter.

Chantal didn't really mind one way or the other. Normally, she would be heading off to the Alps where she managed a lodge for the skiing season, but this year, she had decided to complete the renovation of her newly-purchased cottage in the mountains behind Nice. So the time was unimportant and the cash would come in handy. Also, she was quite curious about this person who could make the usually cautious Serge part with precious euros.

He seemed slightly lost as he stood beside the boat and Jean-Paul rushed to guide him across the gangplank. Chantal was surprised that he was only carrying a backpack as most of their clients arrived with vast amounts of luggage that were a problem to stow. He moved slowly as if burdened with concern.

Without fuss, he chose the first cabin shown to him and indicated that he would rest until dinner. He appeared exhausted and the crew left him in peace.

Chantal had overall management responsibility for the cruise but her main task was as Entertainment Officer. Each day, she would conduct a tour to a place of interest: a winery, a picturesque village or somewhere of historical importance. Despite having done a considerable amount of research into the region and its customs and being in her second season on board the *Clair de Lune*, Chantal felt daunted by the prospect of entertaining such an attractive, single man, who appeared only slightly older than her thirty-something years.

The primary industry of the Languedoc is wine-making and it had been a pleasure for her to become adept at distinguishing between the different local styles and their more celebrated cousins from other parts of France. Their first sortie into the countryside was to a winery that had been in the same family for many generations. Raymond paid close attention as the enthusiastic owner proudly showed his produce. He seemed quite knowledgeable himself and mentioned that, in the dim and distant past, his family had been in the same business. It was when the owner mentioned that the winery was built on the site of an ancient Roman villa and revealed his amateur attempts at archaeological excavations, that Raymond became most animated, displaying the deep understanding and appreciation of classical history born of a good education.

The next day, after they had negotiated a stunning flight of locks, they visited Narbonne and here his mood was to change dramatically from boyish enthusiasm to something approaching despair.

Chantal chose the main square in front of the Hôtel de Ville and the cathedral to introduce Raymond to the story of the Cathars, the Albigensian Crusade and the dramatic events of the thirteenth century that were to end with over half a million dead over two generations.

The Cathars were a mysterious people who appeared in Europe in the eleventh century and are believed to have originated in Persia. They found a welcome in the Languedoc region where the rulers, the Counts of Toulouse, were tolerant of alternative beliefs to the established Roman Catholic religion, including Jews, Muslims and the Cathars. The Cathars believed in living in poverty, in reincarnation and were strict vegetarians. They had no objection to contraception, euthanasia and suicide. The tenet of their faith that ultimately brought them into direct confrontation with the Catholic Church was their refusal to swear oaths and pay tithes; this undermined the feudal system and the power of the Church.

When Pope Innocent III realised that he was losing the propaganda war, he declared a Crusade to stamp out the 'heretics'. The first engagement was at Beziers where twenty thousand men, women and children were massacred. As the soldiers could not distinguish between Cathar and Catholic, they killed indiscriminately on the infamous, chilling instruction of Abbot Arnaud Amaury: 'Kill them all. God will know his own.'

Chantal explained to Raymond that Narbonne was spared as it was the headquarters of the Church in the region. The crusaders moved on to defeat Carcassonne and eventually to remove all trace of the Cathars; a truly monstrous case of genocide.

Raymond listened in sombre silence to Chantal's monologue, occasionally shaking his head in dismay. To her surprise, he angrily refused the opportunity to enter the cathedral, one of the most impressive in France with a complicated history of construction, spread over many centuries.

They met Yves at the market where he was buying the week's provisions but Raymond was in no mood to take an interest and remained silent all the way back to the canal where the trusty *Clair de Lune* awaited them.

Gradually, his good humour returned and, by evening, he was engaging in banter with Chantal as she presented the daily selection of wine for his appreciation. He greeted Yves's customary 'explication' on the evening's menu with relish and later listened intently as Anna explained her choice of cheeses, cheeses that she secretly disliked.

Their next outing took them to the medieval village of Minerve whose location is almost certainly unique. It sits on a ridge which juts out into a narrow ravine, like nature poking out its tongue. A fortress once dominated its summit but this has long since been destroyed and replaced by a close cluster of small dwellings. Chantal parked the van on the other side of the ravine, directly opposite the tip of the ridge and looked back at the village through the rain and mist. It was a magical effect that shed centuries off the scene.

Raymond leant across her to look through the driver's window and she was uncomfortably aware of his warm breath and body heat. Chantal took up the story of the Great Heresy and the

Crusade from where she had left it in Narbonne. Fleeing from Beziers, some one hundred and eighty Cathars were granted sanctuary by Viscount Guilhem in Minerve. The pursuing crusaders, under the leadership of Simon de Montfort, laid siege to the town. She pointed out where they had erected the four huge catapults that had rained rocks onto the fortress. Eventually, Minerve capitulated, more through lack of water than willingness to fight. The villagers were spared but the Cathars chose martyrdom by flinging themselves off the cliffs into waiting fires.

Chantal then told him the most cruel story of the Crusade. Twenty of the surviving villagers were mutilated by having their noses sliced off and their eyes removed, all except one person who had one eye saved and whose responsibility was to lead the others through the countryside, village by village, to demonstrate the futility of resistance and the penalty for harbouring the 'heretics'.

Raymond, who had been silent throughout, muttered quietly, 'Bram.'

'Pardon?' said Chantal.

'I'm sorry to correct you but that last event occurred in Bram, not Minerve.'

It suddenly dawned on Chantal that Raymond had intimate knowledge of the crusade and had just been humouring her, both here and in Narbonne. Horror and embarrassment spread across her face. Realising her distress, Raymond placed a hand on her arm and said, 'Please understand. I know these stories as I have been told them all my life but, by repeating them now with such conviction, you have done me a greater service than you can possibly understand.'

They entered the village and he stood for a long time looking down the *Rue des Martyrs* along which the Cathars took their last fearful, defiant steps. Then, once again, they drove home in silence with Chantal wondering who this man could be.

Their last foray into the countryside was to Lagrasse which is rated as one of the most beautiful villages in France. Reputedly, its abbey was founded by Charlemagne in the eighth century after seeing seven hermits reproduce the miracle of the loaves and fishes but Raymond showed it scant attention, preferring to roam the cobbled streets and appreciate the medieval cottages, recently renovated with English money.

Soon enough, the cruise was over, but not before the crew noticed another strange phenomenon. At each lock, Raymond would step out onto the towpath and chat to each of the lockkeepers who had been summoned from leave to operate the lock gates. A small crowd would also gather to talk to this stranger and the crew noted that word seemed to go ahead of them so that, at each lock, the crowd would be larger. The people treated him with great deference and seemed deeply affected by his presence, a feeling with which Chantal and her friends could readily identify.

Now she watched him disappear into Carcassonne station heading purposefully in an unknown direction, in aid of an unknown cause. In contemplative mood, she turned back to the van and returned to the boat and her colleagues.

A little later, when Serge arrived at the boat, he found them sitting around the dining table, eating their last lunch in companionable silence. As soon as he stepped on board however, he was met with a barrage of questions about the identity of the mysterious Raymond and he realised that his old friend had made quite an impression.

'So you want to know Raymond's story?' said Serge, smiling. 'You may be surprised to learn that you have just entertained the new Count of Toulouse.

'Chantal, you will know that his predecessors were responsible for the protection enjoyed by the Cathars when they immigrated here in the eleventh century, thus incurring the wrath of the Catholic Church. During the following Crusade, the estates of the Counts of Toulouse were confiscated and they were condemned to roam the kingdom penniless. Despite their reduced state, they were highly respected by the common people for their honesty and fairness and they continued to use the power this gave them to protect the few remaining Cathars. They have kept up this tradition all through the centuries and Raymond has just inherited this responsibility. As Cathars, my family have long been beneficiaries of this protection and Raymond and I have known each other since childhood. He turned to me in his concern and confusion at his fate. He did not know if he had the strength of conviction and dedication to lead the simple life this demanded. I have just spoken to him and he told me that his time with you has re-energised him and he is now ready to face the challenges ahead. I don't know what you did or said but it has certainly done the trick and I thank you all.'

Little was Chantal to know that she would never complete her much-anticipated renovations. Within days, a letter would arrive carrying the seal of the Count of Toulouse that would change and enrich her life forever.

TRANSCRIPT

ADVANCED HISTORY PODCAST # 263 –
The Sermon on the Mount by JI

Welcome to my Advanced History podcast number 263 where we will explore the Sermon on the Mount as recorded by the disciple, Matthew.

As my regular subscribers will know, my normal approach is to present all of the available evidence relating to a particular historical event, to analyse that evidence and present a conclusion as to its veracity.

Today, I am taking a different approach and will share with you one of the ways that I prepare for these podcasts in the hope that you will find it of interest. It may be something you enjoy doing yourself and today I will give you the opportunity to participate.

It is a simple three-stage process, employing the disciplines of mediation. As usual, I research all available information sources and decide upon a most likely scenario. Then I enter a meditative state and re-envisage the subject event in detail as a virtual play. This allows me to check the completeness and consistency of my theories.

I have chosen the Sermon on the Mount * for today's topic and I will talk you through my process. For complete openness, I will admit to an ulterior motive. The prime objective is to produce an interesting, accurate account of this event for the podcast but I also intend to use it as a chance to test my personal level of Christian belief.

Over my lifetime, my engagement with religion has been cursory and, at best, I regard myself as agnostic. The Sermon on the Mount is regarded by many as the embodiment of Jesus's teachings, the fundamentals of the Christian faith. I have already completed my research phase and have formulated my most likely scenario so I will be testing it out from both an academic and personal perspective.

Now, we all have to relax and I will take you on a journey through space and time to witness the Sermon.

Most of us have techniques for relaxation so you should use yours if you have one. In my case, I lie down and gradually relax every muscle in my body, starting with the feet and moving up. If I strike a stubborn body part refusing to respond, I go back to the feet and start again. Eventually, I'm in a state whereby I am virtually unaware of my body, my breathing is slow and regular and my consciousness is residing in my head, looking at the back of my eyelids. I've had so much practice I can now do this in seconds. You might like to try this and, if so, I suggest you hit the pause button until you feel ready for the next step.

Now, we get to the interesting part and you may find your imagination stretched to the limit.

I grant myself certain powers which will facilitate the reimagination of the event.

I imagine that I am invisible, that I can fly and that I can travel through time. Lastly, I endow myself with the ability to understand all languages ever spoken by humankind. This allows me to choose any situation, travel immediately to it, hover invisibly over the action and understand everything that's going on. I'd love to be able to take along a silent video recorder but that's taking things a bit too far.

How relaxed are you feeling? Ready to hear the Sermon?

Allow your mind to float free with mine and we find ourselves on the Mount of the Beatitudes in Northern Israel. My research indicates that this is the most likely site for Jesus's delivery of the Sermon.

A crowd has gathered and Jesus, attended by his disciples, is addressing the masses in a clear, golden voice. We are too far back to be able to hear clearly so I am gliding forward, just above the heads of the entranced people until I'm just in front of Jesus. How exciting!

Oops, I've made an error of judgement here and come in too late. Jesus has been speaking for some time.

Hold on, Jesus has paused. He's looking directly at me with some annoyance. Good heavens, he's grabbed me by the collar and is pulling me down. What the–?

'Late again, Judas?'

Transcript Ends
(* See Appendix)

ONE TO WATCH

My wife, Leigh, had booked our son into the local Rugby Tots programme and had instructed me to go along to watch his first game. To be frank when I probably shouldn't, our son had developed into an extremely bright but obnoxious five-year-old and I didn't look forward to spending time with him but I was running short of brownie points at the time so I didn't have a choice.

I hadn't heard of Rugby Tots and Leigh told me that it was a gentle way of introducing youngsters to the sport. Apparently, over fifty-five thousand children attend classes around the world and it's designed to be fun; 'Rugby with a Smile and Passion' is the motto. Apart from basic skills training, the kids play a friendly form of tag rugby and today's match was the culmination of several weekends of tuition. Leigh was hoping that the experience might help socialise the kid.

I have to admit that this didn't sound like adequate preparation for the scary, physical combat of my personal experience but I suspended my scepticism and went along.

I settled myself close to the halfway line and turned my attention to the action on the pitch. I'd seen young children play football before and they never had any idea of 'structure' and 'position'. They would tend to cluster around the ball and follow it around like a swarm of demented bees. Any scores were infrequent and largely accidental.

From the outset, it became apparent that the coaches had done a good job in this department and the opposing sides ran out and scattered into something that vaguely resembled classic formation. It was the 'Reds' versus the 'Blues' and our lad was at fullback for the Reds.

As luck would have it, the Blues' kick-off went straight towards him but, before he could gather it, one of the Blue team wingers swooped on the ball and sprinted through to score. If you'd blinked, you would have missed it. The last thing our young fellow likes is being made to look foolish so he did not take this well.

In accordance with the rules, the Reds restarted play with a kick-off and, after a few fumbling passes, the ball ended up in the hands of the winger and he immediately scored another try. When I say 'immediately', the ball was in his possession one second and he'd planted it triumphantly behind the try line the next. At least, that's how it felt. He was that fast, I christened him 'Bullet'.

Thus the pattern of the game was set. Reds kick off; pass the ball to Bullet; Bullet scores try. Reds kick off. . .

In an attempt to even things up a little, the referee decided to ignore the rules and make the Blues kick off, rather than the Reds, but the result was the same. Bullet had the uncanny ability of recovering the ball directly from the kick-off and scoring without a hand being laid on him.

After ten minutes of this, the Reds lost interest in the proceedings as did the Blues, with the exception of Bullet who ended up playing alone: kicking-off, recovering and scoring. He had the good grace to appear embarrassed by the situation and he didn't seem to notice my son fomenting envy amongst the other players. As I said at the outset, my son was not turning into a nice person.

The talent of Bullet was quite extraordinary and I felt certain that I was watching a future Wallaby, one who had the potential to beat the All Blacks on his own. I'd love to see that.

After the game, I sought out the Head Coach in a state of some excitement.

'Coach, did you watch the Reds versus Blues game? What about that young bloke playing on the wing for the Blues? He scored twenty tries!'

'I did see him as we've had our eye on him since he joined the Tots. It's obvious he's a phenomenal prospect even at his young age.'

'I want to keep an eye on his progress. What's his name?'

'Kent. Clark Kent.'

On the way home, I was singing the praises of young Clark, but my son, Lex, was having none of it. He said he'd cheated. I could tell from the tone of his voice that this story had a long way to run.

Spiders
Snakes
Spiders

MONKEY BRAIN

I've been afflicted with the dreaded writer's block for over twelve months now and my agent, Henry, is getting as frustrated as I am. By nature, Henry is an upbeat character but my continuing lack of output is wearing even him down as I could tell by the tone of his voice when we arranged this meeting. While I regard Henry as a friend after so many years of business association, I am aware that I provide a major portion of his income so he has more than just a personal interest in getting me 'unblocked' and productive again.

In fairness to myself, I have been through a lot over the past year which has caused me a large degree of anxiety, resulting in what I call 'monkey brain'. This is where your mind gets stuck on one thought and goes around and around incessantly. It's impossible to think of anything else while this is happening. I've tried meditation and medication to no avail.

It's the result of an accumulation of issues, starting with a blood clot on my left lung last March. One Friday night, I developed pains in the back and, on a medical friend's advice, I went to the Accident and Emergency department of our local hospital. It took them seven hours of tests to identify the problem and I was admitted for treatment and further tests. As there was a shortage of beds, I was kept in A&E.

Around me, it was total bedlam. Separated from me by a thin curtain, was a young woman who had attempted suicide by inserting electrical cord in her left arm and further along was a seriously inebriated bloke who spent the night groaning and loudly calling for help. Not a peaceful environment.

The only bed to become available overnight was in the oncology ward so off I went to sharc a room with three fellows, all of whom had advanced brain cancer. I felt like an imposter. When the daughter of the bloke opposite enquired as to my condition, I told her, 'It's a blood clot but I'm really quite ill.'

After forty-eight hours of unsuccessful tests to locate the cause of the blood clot, I was discharged. When my wife picked me up, I told her to drive around to the main entrance so I could be admitted as a psychiatric patient. It had been sheer torture.

Over the coming months, I was subjected to every scan and test known to medical science but no cause was found, leaving me with a cloud over my head and a lifetime of blood thinners ahead of me.

In October, my previously diagnosed, early-stage prostate cancer decided to go rogue. It grew in size and threat and demanded to be treated. I opted for radiotherapy over surgery but had to wait several anxious months before my turn came. The treatment was not too uncomfortable but my stress levels went through the roof and I turned to my GP to prescribe anti-anxiety pills.

Just when I thought I was out of the woods, I contracted bronchitis plus Covid. Total joy.

It's now March again and mentally I'm not in good shape. I'm able to sleep alright but, as soon as I wake up, the monkey brain starts and I am unable to put pen to paper, metaphorically speaking.

Henry is sitting opposite me with his elbows on his desk and his head in his hands. I've just completed telling him this tale of woe and it hasn't seemed to have improved his day by much.

He told me he'd been doing some research and had come up with an idea. He asked if I'd heard of 'exposure therapy' and of course, I hadn't. Apparently, the subject is gradually exposed to the source of their anxiety to desensitise them. If you are scared of spiders, for instance, you are gently introduced to spiders and lose your fear.

Henry's idea was for me to confront my anxiety by attempting to write about it. This might exorcise the devil and stop the monkey brain.

It took a number of false starts but, as you will have realised by now, you are reading the result of this experiment. It could be a psychiatric therapy breakthrough.

This is an all-round success. I am less stressed and unblocked and Henry's cashflow is restored or will be once he's sold this story.

INDUCTION

Greetings and welcome to Heaven, Adrian. You're looking a little startled but that's understandable.

You died about three microseconds ago, not that time will have any meaning for you from now on as I'll explain.

How? You tripped over a landmine which I must say was a little careless.

While you regain your wits, let me explain the process from here. I am responsible for inducting you into Heaven. I call it an 'induction' but the more correct term would be 'transformation'; however, people find this a bit confronting.

So, Adrian, now that you've recovered your composure, we should make a start. Your induction will be multiphase and you can complete it at your own pace. We've got an eternity of time ahead of us (and behind us for that matter) so there's no need to rush.

You will note that your body has been reconstituted which, given the landmine episode, took a bit of doing so I hope you appreciate it. This is designed to minimise the panic in newcomers. It's bad enough finding yourself dead without also being disembodied.

But there are some challenges with this. Your Christian version of Heaven was designed around two thousand years ago by gentlemen who were very strong on philosophy and theology but somewhat lacking when it came to town planning. I think they can be excused because little was known at the time about the physical sciences and mathematics were a thing of the future. This is a long way round of saying that the plumbing's poor and there's no electricity.

So, you will be missing most of the mod cons to which you are accustomed in the Twenty-First Century and, to make matters worse, Moses lost the eleventh tablet which said, 'Bring Toilet Paper'.

Why haven't we updated the facilities?

Well, it's not as simple as you might think. The Bible would have to be rewritten which some would regard as sacrilege and this could trigger a mass loss of faith. In this cynical age with already declining numbers, we simply can't afford to lose any more believers.

Look, don't get too worked up about this. This phase will be over quickly and I'm sure you'll survive. In the meantime, I'll organise an emergency supply of papyrus for you.

A word of advice. Contrary to popular belief, new arrivals tend to be less than thrilled about being dead and in Heaven, particularly if their passing has come as a surprise. So to avoid becoming overly depressed, it might be wise to keep to yourself until the general mood begins to improve, which it inevitably will.

Once you feel comfortable, we will move on.

You will part with your body and exist simply as a soul. That's 'simply as a soul', not 'as a simple soul': nothing could be further from the truth.

All of the initial discomforts will fade away and you will experience a euphoric sense of freedom. It's possible that you may even start to think that this is so pleasant that it makes it worth stepping on a landmine. Well, maybe not. Let's see when we get there.

At this stage, you will retain all of your individual characteristics: your sense of humour, your prejudices and your belief system for instance, all the things that make Adrian, *Adrian*. These you will slowly jettison until your soul can be considered 'pure'. Some people find this concept daunting but I can assure you that you will be rewarded by a state of blissfulness, such as that achieved by the Saints of ancient times.

Now, we will begin the most challenging stage.

Imagine that your soul, in essence your consciousness, is inside a cube and it has expanded to completely fill the cube. Now imagine that all six sides of the cube are suddenly removed and your consciousness expands in an instant to fill the Universe, stretching away to infinity in all directions.

We then will go even further and eliminate the concept of time. Everything that has ever happened and everything that will happen will be occurring all at once everywhere in this vast consciousness that you will now possess. Mind blowing stuff, I agree.

Adrian, please don't worry about this now. I'm just trying to give you a sense of what is ahead of you and I'll be with you all of the way.

You will then be ready for all of the knowledge in the Universe to be downloaded into your now infinite, timeless consciousness, at the end of which process you will be fully enlightened.

I know that's a lot to take in so do you have any questions?

Ah, that's another good one. Where does God fit into all of this?

I thought you might have twigged to this by now.

I am God. And when we have finished your transformation, so will you be.

I think that's worth the trip, don't you, Adrian?

Afterword

If *Amusings* made you smile a few times, then its mission is accomplished.

My friend and editor, Mark, was very confident that this would be the case as he made me undertake comprehensive market testing before he would commit to the project.

So I shared my stories with my more erudite family members and here is a selection of their reviews:

'Tolstoy without the humour.'

'Think *Confederacy of Dunces* and then buy that.'

'The comedic influence of Mao's *Little Red Book* shines through.'

'The quality that Douglas Adams aspired to when he was ten.'

'Most acute social commentary since the publication of *Mein Kampf.*'

I was able to convince Mark that this just demonstrated how deeply my family's sense of irony is embedded in our DNA and that these comments should be interpreted as encouraging. I didn't point out that they all said that they wouldn't buy the book. No editor should stand between a wannabe author and his publisher.

So Mark ordered the presses to roll and the bytes to click (Kindle version only).

And finally, a shout out to my mate, huddling in the underground bunker in 3023. I heard you, brother, thanks.

Ian Jackson

List of credits

S, K Taylor, 2023

Please Return When Ready (The Faithless Healer), K Taylor, 2023

Notes For The Senate, K Taylor, 2023

The Last Mini Cooper, K Taylor, 2023

Why You? K Taylor, 2023

Sculpture, Petra Norfolk, 2023

Taking The Tablets, K Taylor, 2023

Anxiety (Monkey Brain), K Taylor 2023

Stormy, Martin Kellard, 2023

Author

Ian Jackson

Ian was born in 1946 in Brisbane, Australia. After an unremarkable childhood in the Brisbane suburb of Chermside where he did not own a cat and once scored 89 not out for the Chermside Methodist Church cricket team, he began a career working in computers with IBM implementing IT systems around the globe. More recently, he has been involved in charitable works, supporting Australian First Nations businesspeople in start-up ventures, setting up a postgraduate training centre for dermatologists in the Pacific Islands and democratising access to dental health services.

He now owns a cat called Stormy.

Contributors

Illustrations – K Taylor

K Taylor is an illustrator, storyboard artist, photographer and *flâneur*, working mainly in TV. Raised by wolves, he taught himself to draw by studying the work of comic artists he admired. In his spare time, he enjoys street photography, peeking round corners and the cutthroat world of competitive croquet. Follow him (please) on Instagram: @kimstadesign

Illustrations – Petra Norfolk

Petra Norfolk is a recent textile design graduate from the University of Leeds. Art has been a passion since she was a young girl and today her art encompasses paints, pencils, embroidery and digital drawings. This year she plans to travel to Rio for the infamous carnival, followed by Bolivia, Peru and Colombia as an important rite of passage before getting a full-time job and settling down to really become an 'adult'.

Illustrations – Martin Kellard

Martin Kellard was creative director and chairman of Australia's largest and most successful advertising agency. He has written a best-selling business book, *Stop Bitching, Start Pitching* and taught presentation techniques to a great many people.

Presently he enjoys reading, writing, drinking wine in the sunshine and drawing in graphite.

Editor – Mark Norfolk

An award-winning playwright and filmmaker, Mark was a writer in residence within a high security prison for a number of years publishing several books of offender writing. He is an associate lecturer in screenwriting at Birkbeck University of London and is currently working with Teatro Internacional De Cabo Verde (TICAVE) helping to establish and develop professional theatre in the tiny west African region.

Editor's Note

Ian Jackson is a foundation director of two Australian charities, Worthwhile Ventures which supports Australian First Nations entrepreneurs and Pacific Dermatology which has established a postgraduate, dermatology training centre in Suva. He is currently working with his niece, Dr. Alexandra Jones on an initiative to address the global inequity of access to dental health care by developing an online education and lifestyle assessment service to empower patients. This project is at the feasibility study stage. He has pledged his royalties from the sale of this book to these or similar charities.

Appendix

Transcript

1 *And seeing the multitudes, he went up into a mountain: and when he was set, his disciples came unto him.*

2 *And he opened his mouth, and taught them, saying:*

3 *Blessed are the poor in spirit: for theirs is the kingdom of heaven.*

4 *Blessed are they that mourn: for they shall be comforted.*

5 *Blessed are the meek: for they shall inherit the earth.*

6 *Blessed are they which do hunger and thirst after righteousness: for they shall be filled.*

7 *Blessed are the merciful: for they shall obtain mercy.*

8 *Blessed are the pure in heart: for they shall see God.*

9 *Blessed are the peacemakers: for they shall be called the children of God.*

10 *Blessed are they which are persecuted for righteousness' sake: for theirs is the kingdom of heaven.*

11 *Blessed are ye, when men shall revile you, and persecute you, and shall say all manner of evil against you falsely, for my sake.*

12 *Rejoice, and be exceeding glad: for great is your reward in heaven: for so persecuted they the prophets which were before you.*

13 *Ye are the salt of the earth: but if the salt have lost his savour, wherewith shall it be salted? it is thenceforth good for nothing, but to be cast out, and to be trodden under foot of men.*

14 *Ye are the light of the world. A city that is set on a hill cannot be hid.*

15 *Neither do men light a candle, and put it under a bushel, but on a candlestick; and it giveth light unto all that are in the house.*

16 *Let your light so shine before men, that they may see your good works, and glorify your Father which is in heaven.*

17 *Think not that I am come to destroy the law, or the prophets: I am not come to destroy, but to fulfil.*

18 *For verily I say unto you, Till heaven and earth pass, one jot or one tittle shall in no wise pass from the law, till all be fulfilled.*

19 *Whosoever therefore shall break one of these least commandments, and shall teach men so, he shall be called the least in the kingdom of heaven; but whosoever shall do and teach them, the same shall be called great in the kingdom of heaven.*

20 *For I say unto you, That except your righteousness shall exceed the righteousness of the scribes and Pharisees, ye shall in no case enter into the kingdom of heaven.*

21 *Ye have heard that it was said by them of old time, Thou shalt not kill; and whosoever shall kill shall be in danger of the judgment:*

22 *But I say unto you, That whosoever is angry with his brother without a cause shall be in danger of the judgment: and whosoever shall say to his brother, Raca, shall be in danger of the council: but whosoever shall say, Thou fool, shall be in danger of hell fire.*

23 *Therefore if thou bring thy gift to the altar, and there rememberest that thy brother hath ought against thee;*

24 *Leave there thy gift before the altar, and go thy way; first be reconciled to thy brother, and then come and offer thy gift.*

25 *Agree with thine adversary quickly, whiles thou art in the way with him; lest at any time the adversary deliver thee to the judge, and the judge deliver thee to the officer, and thou be cast into prison.*

26 *Verily I say unto thee, Thou shalt by no means come out thence, till thou hast paid the uttermost farthing.*

27 *Ye have heard that it was said by them of old time, Thou shalt not commit adultery:*

28 *But I say unto you, That whosoever looketh on a woman to lust after her hath committed adultery with her already in his heart.*

29 *And if thy right eye offend thee, pluck it out, and cast it from thee: for it is profitable for thee that one of thy members should perish, and not that thy whole body should be cast into hell.*

30 *And if thy right hand offend thee, cut it off, and cast it from thee: for it is profitable for thee that one of thy members should perish, and not that thy whole body should be cast into hell.*

31 *It hath been said, Whosoever shall put away his wife, let him give her a writing of divorcement:*

32 *But I say unto you, That whosoever shall put away his wife, saving for the cause of fornication, causeth her to commit adultery: and whosoever shall marry her that is divorced committeth adultery.*

33 *Again, ye have heard that it hath been said by them of old time, Thou shalt not forswear thyself, but shalt perform unto the Lord thine oaths:*

34 *But I say unto you, Swear not at all; neither by heaven; for it is God's throne:*

35 *Nor by the earth; for it is his footstool: neither by Jerusalem; for it is the city of the great King.*

36 *Neither shalt thou swear by thy head, because thou canst not make one hair white or black.*

37 *But let your communication be, Yea, yea; Nay, nay: for whatsoever is more than these cometh of evil.*

38 *Ye have heard that it hath been said, An eye for an eye, and a tooth for a tooth:*

39 *But I say unto you, That ye resist not evil: but whosoever shall smite thee on thy right cheek, turn to him the other also.*

40 *And if any man will sue thee at the law, and take away thy coat, let him have thy cloak also.*

41 *And whosoever shall compel thee to go a mile, go with him twain.*

42 *Give to him that asketh thee, and from him that would borrow of thee turn not thou away.*

43 *Ye have heard that it hath been said, Thou shalt love thy neighbour, and hate thine enemy.*

44 *But I say unto you, Love your enemies, bless them that curse you, do good to them that hate you, and pray for them which despitefully use you, and persecute you;*

45 *That ye may be the children of your Father which is in heaven: for he maketh his sun to rise on the evil and on the good, and sendeth rain on the just and on the unjust.*

46 *For if ye love them which love you, what reward have ye? do not even the publicans the same?*

47 *And if ye salute your brethren only, what do ye more than others? do not even the publicans so?*

48 *Be ye therefore perfect, even as your Father which is in heaven is perfect.*